Ready to Roll!

DONUT dreams

Ready to Roll!

Coco Simon

Simon Spotlight

New York   London   Toronto   Sydney   New Delhi

SIMON SPOTLIGHT
An imprint of Simon & Schuster Children's Publishing Division
1230 Avenue of the Americas, New York, New York 10020
This Simon Spotlight paperback edition May 2021
Copyright © 2021 by Simon & Schuster, Inc.
All rights reserved, including the right of reproduction in whole or in part in any form.
SIMON SPOTLIGHT and colophon are registered trademarks of Simon & Schuster, Inc.
Text by Valerie Dobrow
For information about special discounts for bulk purchases, please contact Simon & Schuster Special Sales at 1-866-506-1949 or business@simonandschuster.com.
Designed by Ciara Gay
The text of this book was set in Bembo Std.
Manufactured in the United States of America 0321 OFF
10 9 8 7 6 5 4 3 2 1
ISBN 978-1-5344-8547-1 (hc)
ISBN 978-1-5344-8546-4 (pbk)
ISBN 978-1-5344-8548-8 (eBook)
Library of Congress Catalog Card Number 2021932623

Chapter One
Rain or Shine

It had been raining the whole week. And it wasn't just a little drizzly, or the kind of week with showers and then bursts of sun, either. It had been raining buckets of hard, cold rain nonstop.

Today, the sky was dark gray and was filled with thick clouds that seemed to hang so low you could almost reach up and swat them. There were puddles everywhere, and everyone was in a sour mood, including me.

Nothing had gone really, really wrong, but it just seemed like nothing was going right, either. I felt a little sad and a little mad, and also like I might yell at someone over nothing.

Usually, Molly and I walked home after school,

but Dad had been picking us up all week so we wouldn't get drenched.

While I liked those few minutes between leaving school and getting home to clear my head a little, there was something nice about looking up and seeing Dad waiting for us, like he used to before we started middle school and started going to and from school by ourselves.

Even though he always parked in the same place, when Dad saw us he blinked his lights twice so we'd know which car was his. It was a little embarrassing, since we were in middle school now and we knew how to find our dad, but it was also a little comforting.

Most parents were on their phones, but I knew Dad was sitting there scanning the kids streaming out of school, and even in a sea of dark umbrellas, he could always pick us out of the crowd right away.

I opened the front passenger-side door and darted into the car.

Molly opened the back door on the other side and jumped in.

"Ugh!" she groaned, getting her umbrella caught in the frame of the door.

"Molly, shut the door!" I yelled.

The rain was coming in sideways and the whole seat was getting wet.

"I'm trying!" she yelled as she threw the umbrella across the back of the car, splattering water everywhere.

Dad sighed and shook his head.

"Hello, you two balls of sunshine!" he said cheerily. "Everyone have a good day?"

"It was okay," I said, and sighed. "Not great."

"I hate this rain," said Molly. "We had PE inside. And soccer practice is indoors this week."

"The trees and the plants and the lakes like the water," said Dad, pulling out of the parking lot.

Dad always believed in seeing the upside of things.

We were all quiet on the way home. The windshield wipers on the car went back and forth furiously, and the rain slammed into the car.

Then Dad's phone dinged and I glanced at it. "It's from Mom," I said, grabbing it.

"Hey!" said Dad. "That's my phone, not yours. You should at least ask before you answer it!"

Then my phone dinged. "Okay," I said. "Now it's Mom on my phone."

Molly's phone dinged too.

"What's up?" asked Dad, sounding a little worried.

"Nans can't pick up Lindsay," I said, reading my screen.

My grandmother, who I call Nans, usually picked up my cousin Lindsay after school. Lindsay's dad, like my mom and my other uncle, Charlie, all work at the Park View Table, or the Park for short, which is the restaurant my grandparents own in town.

My sisters and cousins also do shifts at the Park. Molly and my older sister, Jenna, work on "the floor," as they say, busing tables, taking orders, cleaning up spills, and waiting tables, like my older cousins Rich and Lily.

I'm pretty lucky because I work at Donut Dreams, which is the donut counter inside the restaurant, with Lindsay. I don't mention this to any of them, but I think Lindsay and I have the easier job just minding the Donut Dreams counter.

"Tell Mom we've got it," said Dad, turning around the block and pulling back into the school lot.

The line of cars had already left, even in that short time, so we drove right up to the entrance.

Lindsay was waiting there with her huge knapsack and a big pink umbrella with rainbows all over it. I felt bad because she was the last one waiting, alone.

Her mom had died two years ago, and since then the whole family has pitched in to help Uncle Mike, Lindsay, and her younger brother, Skylar. Nans and Grandpa live really close by, so there's always someone around, but still, it's times like these that it feels like she's missing someone.

Dad flicked the lights at Lindsay. "Here we are," he called, even though she couldn't hear him from outside the car.

I knew then that he was thinking the same thing I was. I looked over at him and smiled.

Lindsay opened the back door and slid in. "Thanks, Uncle Chris," she said. "Ugh, there's a puddle on this seat."

"Molly did it," I said.

"It was an accident," Molly said dramatically.

"Oh, that's right, Molly had an accident," I said. "On the seat." I started to giggle.

"What kind of accident?" Lindsay asked, grinning mischievously.

"You know what kind," I said, turning around.

"You are kidding!" said Molly. "Stop taunting me!"

"Molly, you *said* you had an accident," I said.

"Not *that* kind of accident!" she yelled.

"Girls, I am driving a car in the middle of a rainstorm," Dad said, even though he was trying not to laugh.

"I did not pee on the seat!" said Molly.

"Okay," I said, laughing.

"I didn't!" she screeched.

"If you did," I said, "then it would be Lindsay who was sitting in it."

"Eeeewww!" cried Lindsay.

"Dad, make her stop!" yelled Molly.

"Okay, enough," said Dad, pulling into our driveway.

After Dad parked the car, he glanced down at his phone, reading messages from my mom.

"Linds, you'll stay here until Nans can swing around and take you home, okay?" he said.

Lindsay paused, and Dad jumped in. "Skylar is all set hanging out at his friend Trevor's house."

"Oh, okay," said Lindsay, looking relieved.

I wondered if I would worry about Molly if she was younger than I was. We were basically the same age, only Molly was eight months older, a fact she liked to remind me of often.

"Okay, let's hurry into the house carefully," said Dad. "Ready, set, race!"

We flung open the car doors and ran to the back door of the house, hurrying in through the mudroom, where Dad had built cubbies for all of us to store our coats and bags.

We dumped our wet stuff and headed into the kitchen, stopping to say hello to our dog, Rusty.

"Snackeroo time!" said Dad, opening up the refrigerator.

Rusty trotted to the fridge behind Dad.

"You too, Rusty," Dad added, as he took out some dog treats.

People think that since our family owns a restaurant, we always have an open kitchen, with tons of stuff coming out of it. But of course we don't. We just have a normal kitchen with mostly normal stuff.

Dad's the one who does most of the cooking in our house, and he makes delicious meals, but it's not like, *Hey, let's order this right now.* We don't have menus propped up on the walls or anything.

Still, Dad can get pretty creative with his after-school snacks.

"For a gloomy day, I think we need something to

cheer us up," said Dad. "Something . . . sunny."

"Sunny-side-up eggs?" asked Lindsay.

"No way," said Molly.

"When I think of sunny, I think of citrus," said Dad.

"Lemons?" I asked.

"Sure," said Dad. "But also these."

He rolled out four clementines from the fridge. Clementines are like little oranges, and they don't have seeds.

"Clementines?" asked Molly, kind of disappointed.

"Yes," said Dad. "And what makes everything better?"

"Chocolate!" I said.

"Bingo!" said Dad. "Stand back and watch."

He handed us each a clementine and told us to peel it and section it.

Then he took a bar of dark chocolate and started melting it in a saucepan on the stove, adding a 1/4 cup of sugar. He dipped each of the sectioned pieces of fruit into the melted chocolate.

He grabbed a handful of shelled pistachio nuts. He smashed the nuts into pieces with a rolling pin, then rolled the chocolate-dipped clementine sections in them. Then he arranged everything on a plate and threw it into the freezer.

"Snack in five minutes!" he said, setting the timer.

We basically just sat around for five minutes, waiting and staring at the freezer, until Dad pulled the plate back out.

The chocolate had set, so it wasn't drippy anymore.

"Some sunshine in the form of a clementine," said Dad. "Hey, that rhymes! A clementine dipped in chocolate is the cure-all for anything gloomy. If you can't have sunshine, then sometimes you need to make it."

"Wow," said Lindsay. "At my house I usually get apple slices and graham crackers."

"Well," I said, biting into the delicious snack and feeling warm and cozy and much better than I had all day, "you're in the right house. Because Dad always knows how to make everything sunny."

Chapter Two
Home Run

It was *still* raining on Friday, when Dad dropped me off after school for my shift at Donut Dreams. My wet sneakers squeaked on the tiled floor of the restaurant when I walked in.

"Wait!" said Grandpa commandingly.

Grandpa was either roaming the restaurant, doing things like chatting with customers or refilling coffee cups, or he was at his post at the podium.

Today, he was at the post.

"Wipe your feet, young lady," he said sternly.

I backed up to the mat in front of the door and wiped my feet.

Grandpa nodded. "Now," he said, "will you give your grandfather a hug?"

I gave him a hug as Mom rounded the corner.

Mom was the accountant for the Park and she was usually in the office, which was next to the kitchen.

She definitely had a special radar. The minute one of us walked into the Park, she made a beeline out of her office to see us.

"Hello, donut crew!" she sang.

I half smiled. I was still grumpy about all the rain.

"This weather still has you blue, doesn't it?" asked Mom, giving me a hug.

I nodded. It wasn't like I wasn't doing things because of the rain. I still went to school, I still went to work. But I was in what Mom called "a funk." It means you feel out of sorts.

"Is there anything that might cheer you up today?" asked Mom. "How about a donut?"

"Eating the profits!" bellowed Grandpa.

"Well," I said, "maybe it's just testing for quality control."

He grinned. "You, my dear, are a smart cookie."

"Do smart cookies get smart donuts?"

Grandpa could be strict at the restaurant, but he always had a soft spot for me. My cousins teased me about it.

"If it will make my granddaughter smile like that, then she can have whatever she wants," said Grandpa.

Then he looked at his watch. "As long as you eat it in ten minutes. Because that's when your shift starts."

I gave him a quick peck on the cheek and headed back to the kitchen.

We had lockers in the kitchen, where we kept clean aprons, gloves, and hair stuff, because you always had to wear your hair off your face if you were serving food.

Before I put on my gloves, I went over to the counter, where Nans had the trays of fresh donuts waiting to be put out in the display cases.

Lindsay was already in the kitchen, with a glass of water and an apple.

I nodded toward the tray. "Grandpa said we could have one."

"Ooh, he did?" asked Lindsay.

She swooped in and grabbed a donut with vanilla frosting and sprinkles on top.

"Better than an apple?" I joked.

"You have to try this," Lindsay said with a grin.

12

"It's our new flavor. Nans named it Sprinkle Surprise."

She bit into the donut and held it out for me to see. The inside was filled with different-colored sprinkles.

"My first thought," I said, breaking one in half, "is how many sprinkles we're going to have to sweep up after serving these."

Lindsay laughed. "Yeah, let's hope most of the ones we sell are to-go."

They were messy but delicious. They tasted a little like vanilla birthday cake.

Lindsay glanced at the clock behind me. "Game time," she said, and we straightened our aprons and headed out to the counter.

When it's raining, there aren't as many customers in the restaurant. People don't like to come out in bad weather, especially toward the end of the day.

While I was relieved that we wouldn't have a lot of crowds, being bored at work is the worst. We aren't supposed to have our phones, per Grandpa's orders, so after we clean and tidy up, we have to kind of just stand around and look busy.

But just then a woman came over with a sad-looking little boy.

DONUT DREAMS

I wiped my hands on my apron and smiled at the two of them.

"Hi!" I said. "Can I help you?"

"We need two delicious 'cheer us up' donuts, don't we, honey?" the woman said.

The boy nodded, his eyes on the floor.

"He had a bad day at the ballpark yesterday," the woman explained. "And he was hoping to make up for it today, but today's game was canceled because of the rain."

She lowered her voice to a whisper. "He struck out twice."

"Three times, Mom!" the little boy shouted. "I struck out three times, not twice."

"Oh man," I said, leaning in. "That stinks. You definitely need a little pick-me-up."

I looked at the donuts in our counter and then back at the boy.

"What's your favorite flavor?" I asked him.

"Chocolate," he said.

I nodded. I took a donut out of the case and showed it to him, as if it were a precious gemstone.

"This is a double chocolate Donut Dreams specialty," I told him. "Chocolate icing, chocolate sprinkles, and when you bite into it, chocolate cream. Guaranteed to make you feel as if you hit a home run. Or at the very least, that you'll hit a home run your next time up at bat."

He wouldn't look at me, but I could see the corners of his mouth turn up a little.

"Is that the beginning of a smile?" I asked. I put the donut in a napkin so he could hold it. "Go on, take a bite," I said. "Let me know what you think."

He looked up at his mom, who nodded. He took a bite. He swallowed. Then he smiled.

"I guess I do feel a little better," he said.

"Sold!" his mother said with a relieved little laugh. "I'll have one too, and a coffee, please."

As I rang up the order, she silently mouthed the words, *Thank you!* to me.

As the two now-happy customers left, I turned to Lindsay with a smile.

"Another crisis avoided!" I said.

Lindsay grinned back.

"Sweep or wipe?" she asked.

We have to wipe down the glass counters constantly, since all the kids—and a lot of adults, too—put fingerprints all over them. And Grandpa freaks out if there are crumbs on the floor, so we're always sweeping, too.

Lindsay and I usually trade off sweeping and wiping, and then we bargain over who will take out the trash.

Trash duty is the worst because people throw all sorts of gross stuff in the trash can. Plus, we have to dump it in the Dumpster in the back of the restaurant, then rinse out the trash can with a hose at the end of the day. Even though we use trash can liners, the liners tear sometimes and stuff leaks out.

That thing can really stink!

"I'll wipe," I said, and I picked up the cloth and the spray bottle.

As I was bending down in front of the case, wiping smudgy thumbprints, I noticed the donuts were a little difficult to see. They were angled so that you couldn't really tell what kind of icing was on top of them unless you knelt way down.

I stood up and squinted, then went behind the counter.

"Hey, Linds," I called. "Let's redecorate."

Lindsay went in front of the counter while I tipped the tray up.

"Can you see them better now?" I asked.

"Oh yeah, that's definitely better," she said. "Wait—maybe space them out more."

She came around the counter. We found a box we could use to prop up the trays. Then we worked to stack up the donuts by type, fanning them across the case.

I also stacked a few on top of the counter on a cake stand. They kind of looked like a tiered wedding cake. We couldn't sell those after being out, but I figured it was just a few, so it was okay.

Plus, it looked really cool.

"A donut cake!" said Lindsay.

"Right?" I said. "We have to be careful though, because the prettiest donuts are going to get ruined by the stacking; you know, the frosting will get smushed, the sprinkles will get all over the place…"

"I guess that's why donuts are usually displayed on trays," Lindsay said with a sigh. "Still, it's fun to do this once in a while as a promotion."

We took some of the flowers out of the vase that was next to the cash register and placed them between the trays in the case, careful not to put them next to the donuts, which would have been a no-no. The flowers were just for decoration.

It took us a little while of rearranging the flowers to figure out which position was the best. We kept going back and forth so many times Grandpa came over to see what was going on, his hands crossed behind his back.

"Hey!" he said. "That case looks fantastic! And what is that?"

Grandpa is full of love for his grandchildren, but he's also not easily impressed. He stood there, nodding.

"Mike!" he called out to my uncle, Lindsay's dad.

Uncle Mike, who's in charge of Donut Dreams, came over, and I could tell he thought we'd done something wrong and Grandpa was going to "show us by example," which is one of his favorite sayings.

But Uncle Mike stopped short too.

"Wow!" he said. "Did you girls do that?"

We nodded.

"That's a work of art!" Uncle Mike exclaimed. "It's beautiful!"

"Look at that donut cake!" said Grandpa. "It's a tower of donuts but a cake!"

A couple of the waiters and waitresses came over, and soon there was a little crowd.

"It looks almost too pretty to eat," said my cousin

Lily, who had just arrived for her job as host.

She usually took customers to their tables and made sure that everyone was seated in a way that didn't overwhelm one waitperson.

"That's not good," said Grandpa, frowning. "But she has a point. What happens when you take out two donuts from that cake?"

"The idea is that you serve it to everyone at once, for a party. Or you could just start at the top layer and eat your way down from there," I said.

I looked at Lindsay, who shrugged. I hadn't thought that far ahead.

Grandpa nodded thoughtfully. "That makes sense," he said. "You wouldn't buy a donut cake for just one person."

"That gives me an idea," said Uncle Mike. "What if we put that on the catering menu? You could order them for birthdays and other celebrations."

"I love it!" said Grandpa. He beamed. "See what we have here? A slow rainy day with not a lot of customers, but my wonderful family is coming up with new business ideas!"

We laughed. I whipped out my phone to take a picture, so we could do it exactly the same way again.

"I'm so happy I'm going to ignore that you had a phone while working, my dear," said Grandpa.

"It's for work purposes!" I protested, but I knew he'd nailed me.

Still, I took a few snaps of the donut stack and the counter. The pictures looked even better than the donuts did in real life.

"I love a rainy day!" Grandpa said, whistling and strolling toward the kitchen.

I definitely did not love a rainy day, but I had to admit, this one wasn't terrible.

Chapter Three
Donut Refill!

On Saturday the weather was absolutely beautiful. And while I was very happy to wake up to the sun, I was not too happy to have to go to work inside on the first bright morning in days.

Saturdays at Donut Dreams were always busy. Uncle Mike did the "early bird" crew from six a.m., when the Park opened, until eight o'clock, when Lindsay and I started.

He stayed with us if things were really crazy, and I had a feeling today would be one of those days.

"Look who brought the sunshine!" said Nans, as she kissed me on the cheek.

She was looking over the specials menus in the kitchen. She set all the specials each week depending on what was in season—apple pie in the fall, for instance—or celebrations like Valentine's Day or the Fourth of July.

Sometimes specials are just based on what we have extra of that week.

One time we had an accidental extra delivery of broccoli. So there was a broccoli quiche on the menu one night, broccoli soup the next, stir-fried broccoli, broccoli with fried rice, then pasta and broccoli.

By the time she got to something that she was calling broccoli sauce, everyone said it was enough with the broccoli specials.

"Nans, those Sprinkle Surprise donuts were so good," I said, glancing around to see if there were any left.

Nans smiled. "Oh, I'm glad you liked them," she said. "I think those will be good to get into the regular baking schedule. The last batch we had is in the case already. I'll make one more so we can get through the morning rush."

I gave her a thumbs-up, tied my apron behind my back, and headed out to the counter.

Lindsay was finishing up with a customer.

"You sent my dad into such a state," said Lindsay,

when she finished bagging up the donuts and waited for the man to leave.

Per Grandpa's rules, we weren't supposed to have a conversation in front of customers.

"You have conversations *with* the customers," Grandpa would say. "You don't speak in *front* of them or *over* them. It's rude!"

"What did I do?" I asked, trying to remember if I rinsed out the trash can yesterday. I thought I had.

"He thinks the donut cake is the next big thing. He's obsessed."

"Huh," I said, tilting my head. "Maybe . . ." I grabbed a few donuts.

"What are you doing?" asked Lindsay.

"Give me a sec," I said, as I started to build a new tower.

I made this donut cake wider and taller than the one I'd made yesterday. It kind of looked more like a wedding cake.

Then I looked around. I remembered the tower we made yesterday had flowers for decoration. We always had fresh flowers in big vases in the front of the Park in addition to little vases on each table.

I skittered over and grabbed a few long stems of

purple flowers, then inserted them in the hole in the middle of the donut pile.

Purple is one of my favorite colors so I was excited to see how this would look. The flowers on top looked like big blooms of icing coming out of the cake.

"That looks amazing!" said Lindsay. "You really have a knack for this!"

Just then Uncle Mike came out of the kitchen carrying a large tray of donuts on his shoulder.

He lowered it onto the counter and said, "Good morning, Kelsey! Here's another batch of Sprinkle Surprise to keep you girls going!"

Lindsay and I started taking the donuts off the tray and arranging them in the case, working quickly. Before we could finish, we had a small line of customers, and the next hour was a rush of Uncle Mike bringing out more donuts, me taking the orders and bagging them, and Lindsay ringing up each purchase.

Finally, we had a break.

"Ugh," said Lindsay. "That was a rush!"

"We're almost out again," I said, counting how many donuts were left. "I'll go let your dad know."

"Seriously?" said Uncle Mike when I poked my head into the kitchen and called, "Donut refill needed!"

He put down his coffee and picked up another tray of donuts.

"Mom, you're killing it with these Sprinkle Surprise donuts," he told Nans.

"The nice weather is finally bringing people back," said Nans.

"Sun is good for sales!" said Uncle Mike, and I followed him back out.

When we got to the counter, Mrs. Silber, who lived down the street from us, was standing there with her daughter, Zoe, who was hopping around and pointing and yelling, "I want *that*!"

"What can we get you?" asked Uncle Mike, placing the tray down.

"Oh," said Mrs. Silber. "She wants that donut cake!"

"It's my birthday soon!" said Zoe.

"Actually," said Mrs. Silber, "your birthday is a month away."

"Yeah, soon!" said Zoe.

Lindsay and I tried not to giggle.

"And I want a donut cake for my birthday. With purple flowers like that!" said Zoe.

"I told her it was just a display," Mrs. Silber said.

Uncle Mike looked at the cake. "Oh!" he said. "That's . . ." He thought for a second. "If you're interested, we could try it. It would be our first one."

Mrs. Silber looked at Zoe. "Is that what you want?" she asked.

"Yes!" Zoe squealed. "I want a donut cake with purple!"

"You can't actually eat those flowers," said Uncle Mike, pointing to the ones I'd put on top. "You'd get a pretty big stomachache. But maybe we could pipe some icing that will look like purple flowers on top."

"Oh, that would be pretty!" said Mrs. Silber. "They'd be flowers made out of frosting, Zoe!"

Zoe beamed.

"Let me know when you want to order it," said Uncle Mike, "and we can figure out what kinds of donuts and how big the cake will be, depending on how many guests you have."

Mrs. Silber bought a dozen donuts to take home and left with a very happy Zoe.

"Look at that!" said Uncle Mike. "In less than

twenty-four hours we've launched a new donut cake business! We're rolling!"

I smiled. "Good for us!"

"Yes," said Uncle Mike. "And you're my secret weapon, because you came up with the idea. But now you have to get this past the finance person to make sure this is a good business decision."

"You mean Mom?" I asked.

"Yep," said Uncle Mike. "And she can be tough. We'll have to figure out how much it will cost us to make, how much we'll charge for it, and how many we think we can make and deliver per week."

"And also how to let people know about them," said Lindsay. "Unless we do a fresh one each week and leave it on the case and just hope people see it and ask about it."

"Exactly," said Uncle Mike. "When we add new items to the catering menu, we usually advertise them, although we'll have to figure out the best way to do that, too. Grandpa is not exactly supportive of social media."

"He hates phones," said Lindsay. "Would he even know if we posted about it?"

That was true. Grandpa did not have a phone,

even though all his children begged him to get one just for safety if his car broke down or he got hurt. Hard pass from Grandpa.

The Park had a website, but it didn't do much; it just had a link to the menu and listed the address and phone number and hours for the restaurant. It also had a very embarrassing picture of my entire family, all in Park aprons, sitting on the front steps, although thank goodness it was from many years ago.

"No, no," said Uncle Mike. "We don't do business like that. Everything gets decided by the Park management team. There are a lot of logistics to figure out. But let's start with the first step. I need to pull together a plan. We have one month until Zoe's birthday party."

"In terms of launching a new business, Zoe might be right," said Lindsay. "One month is pretty soon."

Chapter Four
When Life Gives You Cakes . . .

I only worked two days a week, Fridays and Saturdays. So I woke up on Sunday with the whole day ahead of me. Yesterday's sun had made everyone especially cheery. I pulled up my bedroom shade. It was raining. Again.

I sighed, slid my feet into my slippers, and padded downstairs. Molly was sipping from a glass of orange juice at the table, and Mom and Dad were making pancakes and eggs.

I sniffed.

"What smells so good?"

"Coffee!" said Mom. "Good morning, sweetie!"

"I think you smell bacon," said Dad, standing over a sizzling pan.

Rusty was nuzzling Dad's leg. He was pretty good about not asking people for food, but that dog sure loved bacon.

I sat down at the table and yawned, then looked at Rusty.

"I walked him already," said Dad.

"Whew," I said, slumping back down.

"Do you have any homework you need to finish up today?" asked Mom.

"Mom!" I groaned. "I've been up for ten minutes!"

Mom gave me a look. "Okay, Kelsey," she said slowly. "We'll keep it to gentle, light conversation until you have fully arrived at an alert state this morning."

Molly smirked.

I didn't think it was too much to ask for a little peace and quiet first thing in the morning, especially on a Sunday. I was out of sorts and I didn't know why.

Jenna was sleeping in, Mom and Dad were talking softly to each other—probably murmuring about me—and Molly was reading a book. The only sound was the *splat, splat, splat* of the rain against the window.

I wandered into the family room and grabbed my phone. We had to leave our phones in the charging dock downstairs before we went upstairs to sleep for the night, even my older sister Jenna, who's in high school.

Jenna said it was the dumbest, most unfair rule ever. Mom and Dad said they'd put their phones there too for the night, so the rule was meant for the whole family, and that kind of ended the argument. Sometimes late at night, when most of us were asleep already, you could hear them all dinging.

I already had about thirty-eight texts today, mostly from Sophia, Michelle, and Riley, who have been my best friends since even before kindergarten.

Now that we're in middle school, we've been hanging out more with other kids too, like Olivia and Isabella.

Mom always says, "Additions are better than subtractions" when it comes to friends, so while I miss the tight "just us" group, I've been trying to roll with the larger crew.

The last text was, *Kelsey that is SO AMAZING,* and it had about forty emojis next to it, so I knew it was from Sophia.

Wait, what was amazing?

I scrolled through all the responses until I saw that Lindsay had sent around a picture of the donut cake

31

from yesterday at Donut Dreams. She'd captioned it, *Look what my cousin Kelsey created when she was bored!*

I smiled.

"Oh, is that a smile I see on Ms. Grouchy's face?" asked Dad, leaning in the doorway.

I looked up. "Yes," I said, and waved the phone in front of him, showing him the picture.

"Cool!" said Dad. "Did you find that online?"

"NO!" I said. "I made that at Donut Dreams yesterday!"

Dad grabbed the phone and looked closer.

"Wow!" he said. "That's very cool, Kelsey."

Mom peeked around the corner.

"What's so cool?" she asked. "Weren't you going to tell Kelsey breakfast is ready?"

She wiped her hands on her apron and Dad held up the phone.

"Oh!" she said. "Yeah, that's a neat idea."

"It was Kelsey's idea," said Dad. "She made this at Donut Dreams yesterday."

Mom looked at the phone again.

"Wow," she said. "That's pretty amazing. And that's what Mike was talking about. He was going on and on last night about this great new idea for catering for parties. You know my brother with a new idea."

"We actually have an order already," I said. "Mrs. Silber ordered a cake for Zoe's birthday party."

"That's great!" said Mom. "A donut cake is perfect for a birthday party because each person just gets one donut. You don't have to slice up a cake. There's nothing worse than the pressure of cutting up a cake really fast when kids are waiting for it."

Dad laughed. "Oh, I remember a certain ice cream cake debacle one year for Molly."

Mom moaned. "It was so awful. All the kids were screaming for the ice cream cake, and it was too frozen to cut through."

Dad was laughing. "Yep, we didn't know you had to let it sit out for a while before you served it. We were basically sawing through the thing as fast as we could, and just scooping these crazy pieces onto plates and passing them out."

"It's funny now," said Mom. "At the time, not so much."

"I think I kind of remember that," I said. "Didn't Grandpa do something to it?"

Mom burst out laughing.

"He shoved the whole thing into the oven and

swore that they'd done this at the restaurant before." She shook her head.

"It melted," said Dad. "So then we threw it back in the freezer."

"And then we just gave up," said Mom.

"Hey!" called Molly from the kitchen. "I remember that. And it's still not funny! I had bowls of ice cream soup instead of cake!"

Mom covered her face.

"Ugh," she said. "Yeah, that was an epic cake fail."

"So with the donuts," I said, "you let the birthday kid take the one off the top, then each kid just gets an individual donut. No cutting!"

"And no having the pressure of making sure each piece is exactly the same!" said Dad.

"Or that one kid gets a certain part of the icing on top," I said, "because all the donuts are the same."

"Okay, but we can do donut cakes with all different kinds if someone wants one," Dad said.

"Of course," I said.

"You always try to get the piece with the most icing," yelled Molly.

"I do not!" I said.

"Okay, okay," said Mom. "No fighting! Save those

great points for the marketing plan. Now it's time for breakfast!"

We went back into the kitchen, and Dad put a plate of pancakes on the table.

"Wait a sec," I said.

Everyone watched me as I took the pancakes and stacked them, first in a circle, then on top of each other, stacking them higher. It was a good thing that Dad always made a ton of pancakes, because pretty soon they were like a big stacked cake. I grabbed a few strawberries and placed them around the pancakes, then placed the biggest one on top.

Dad looked on, then handed me the canister we used for sprinkling powdered sugar.

I nodded, then sprinkled the sugar on the pancake tower. It looked like the pancake cake was sprinkled with a little dusting of snow.

"That almost looks too good to eat," said Mom.

"Almost," said Molly, grabbing a fork and trying to stab a pancake.

"WAIT!" I screamed.

I ran to get my phone and snapped a picture.

"Are you done with the professional photo shoot of my breakfast?" asked Molly sarcastically.

"Yeah, I got it," I said.

"You really have a knack for this," said Dad, grabbing a few pancakes and passing the platter to Mom.

"Don't tell my father," said Mom, laughing. "He'll have you styling every single thing in the restaurant."

I thought about that for a second, then sent the picture to my friend group before texting, *When I have rainy days, I do what anyone would do . . . turn things into cakes.*

Chapter Five
One Big Sigh

The week was dreary again. It wasn't pouring rain every day, but there was this lingering drizzle that felt like someone was spitting on you.

It was gross.

And then there was Rusty. Mom and Dad warned us when we got a dog that we'd need to take turns walking him and scooping poop.

We got him when it was warm and sunny and the days were long. It was nice to have time outside, with a dog who wasn't annoyingly asking you about your day or bugging you about borrowing a sweater.

Walking Rusty when it was cold and rainy and dark was a whole other situation. It was not delightful.

Monday morning meant it was my turn to take

Rusty out. Even he didn't seem to want to go out in this weather.

"C'mon, buddy," I said. "Just down the block and back and we're done."

He whined and sat on the front step. I sighed and waited.

"I'm as crabby as you are, boy," I said. "I don't want to do this either."

He seemed to understand me because he got up, walked to the end of the block, did his business, and we trotted home.

If there's any way to tell whether a dog truly loves you, it's that he only pees when you take him out, and that he waits to poop until it's your sister's turn.

※　※　※　※　※

The morning at school went by quickly and was uneventful. After lunch, we filed into English class, which I usually liked, but I still couldn't shake the blah state that I was in.

Since it was so gray outside, the fluorescent lights in the classroom made everything look a little bit glowy and kind of spooky.

"Okay," said Ms. Parkour, our English teacher,

when we all settled in. "I see we're all looking a little gloomy today."

I looked around. Maybe it wasn't just me.

"This weather gives us what I call the blahs," said Ms. Parkour. "As in, you don't feel terrible, and it's just a little rain, but you just don't feel happy, either."

I nodded.

"And I think the best thing for feeling kind of icky is to try to articulate your feelings more by writing," said Ms. Parkour. "So before we dive into today's lesson, your homework for the next two weeks is to start a blog. You don't have to publish it, of course, but try to construct something that expresses how you feel each day."

"Like a journal?" asked Riley.

"A lot of blogs are like journals, right?" said Ms. Parkour. "Many of them are accountings of what the person did that day, and how they felt about it."

Emma raised her hand. "So does it just have to be words or can it be a picture?" she asked.

"Well," Ms. Parkour replied. "I really want you to work on expressing yourself through writing, but that's a good point. Expression can come in many forms, including visual ones."

"Like I could post a great meme that captures exactly how I feel!" said Eric.

Ms. Parkour nodded. "That's why memes are popular, right? Because they capture a feeling in one image that so many people relate to."

"I thought they were popular because they were funny," said Eric, and everyone laughed.

"Okay," said Ms. Parkour, ignoring him. "Let's amend the assignment then. You can absolutely use visual images. But with a visual image, you need to come up with at least one word that summarizes that image."

"I don't get it," said Eric.

"Let's say you post a meme about . . ." Ms. Parkour trailed off.

"Oh, like this one!" Eric said, waving his phone in the air.

"Eric, I'm going to pretend you didn't bring your phone to class," said Ms. Parkour, "or I'll need to take it from you and turn it in to the office."

Eric looked freaked out and stuffed his phone into his knapsack. "No, no, no," he said. "No phone here. I was just illustrating the idea of using a meme."

We all giggled.

"Instead of a meme," Ms. Parkour said, "let's think of an image. Someone give me an idea, please."

"A rainbow!" said Riley.

"A puppy!" said Isabella.

"A sunny day!" said Eric.

"Let's go with the puppy," said Ms. Parkour, heading to the whiteboard at the front of the room.

"Now give me a word that sums up how you might be feeling if you were expressing yourself with a picture of a puppy."

"Cute!" said Isabella.

"Are you trying to express that you are cute or the puppy is cute?" asked Ms. Parkour. "See, that's the difference. I need you to not just summarize the image, but tell me how it relates to *you*!"

"My favorite thing in the world?" said Riley.

"Close!" said Ms. Parkour. "Because you're telling me what your relationship is to the puppy. But take that a little further. How does it make you feel when you see that puppy or when you're with that puppy?"

"Whoa, that's deep," said Eric.

Ms. Parkour laughed. "It doesn't have to be that deep," she said, "unless you want it to be. This exercise is about using words for self-expression."

"How about 'safe'?" said Isabella.

"Aha!" said Ms. Parkour. "So if I'm looking at the picture and I see that your word is 'safe,' then I'm going to assume that you feel safe and comforted and peaceful with that puppy. Is that right?"

"Yes!" said Isabella.

"There you go," said Ms. Parkour. "Okay, it seems like we're onto something here, so let's change course with our plans. Instead of diving into the original lesson—which, by the way, was about what a sonnet is—let's stay with this. Everyone take out a notebook or a tablet or laptop. If you'd rather stick to just words, that's great. If you want to use or think of an image, that's okay too. But let's focus on how we're feeling today, and we can get your homework for tonight done in class."

"Yes!" yelled Eric, as he pumped his fist. "No homework makes me happy. My word is 'happy'!"

"I'm glad what you're feeling today will be happy," said Ms. Parkour. "For everyone else, think of how you really feel, and try to boil it down to words or images. Actually, you don't even have to boil it down. If you want to write ten pages expressing yourself, that's fine too."

"Ten pages!" yelped Eric. "I can do it in one!"

"As long as that one page really captures how you feel, that's fine," said Ms. Parkour. "Use the number of words you need. Some days will be long and some may be short, but I'd like you to do this every day for two weeks. You can take one day off on the weekend."

The class was quiet. A lot of kids started writing right away. Ms. Parkour walked around, softly talking to kids and helping some of them get going.

Riley was sitting next to me and was writing furiously, biting her lip. I knew when she did that move, she was really concentrating.

I looked out the window. How *did* I feel?

I felt . . . icky. Icky meant that I didn't feel terrible, but I didn't feel great. I started writing down words:

Icky

Blech

Blah

I looked out the window. I sighed. Actually, that was it. That was how I felt, so I wrote it down:

Today, I feel like one big sigh.

Chapter Six
Donut Test Drive

As we were getting ready for dinner that night, Mom said, "Kelsey, your donut cake was the buzz of the restaurant today."

"It was?" I asked, collecting the silverware to set the table. "Who was buzzing about it?"

"Uncle Mike, Grandpa, and Uncle Charlie," said Mom, pouring water into everyone's glass. "And of course, Nans and I were in on it too."

"What was the discussion?" I asked.

Mom grabbed her phone. "Look," she said. "I have some pictures and some videos."

We sat down at the half-set table.

"If we do these cakes, we can offer them in two sizes," Mom said. "You can't really do a tiny cake because you need a certain number of donuts to get some heft and some height to it."

I looked at the photos. There were two versions side by side, one like the one I had created and one giant one that looked like it had a hundred donuts.

"Uncle Charlie figured out that we can order dowels," said Mom.

"Dowels?" I said.

"They're long sticks that bakers sometimes use in tiered cakes. They get plunged straight through so they help keep the cakes steady and held together. When you see a giant cake rolled out at a wedding or a party, they usually have dowels in them, but you can't see them. When they're ready to cut and serve the cake, they take them out."

"Huh," I said. "Having those would have helped me steady that thing."

"Right?" said Mom.

"Hey, what's that?" I asked, as Mom flipped through the pictures.

"That's what Nans thought we could do," said Mom. "Pretty, right?"

The photo was a donut cake like I'd done, only instead of real flowers, Nans had made them out of

45

frosting. She had also piped in icing between each stack, so there were frosted rings around the donuts.

"That looks beautiful!" I said. "So good you could eat it."

"We also ordered some larger cake trays so we can use them as the base to build these on. The cake trays we have aren't wide enough."

I nodded. I had just placed them on a platter.

We didn't make birthday cakes to go at the restaurant, but if someone asked, Grandpa would do a special order, as he called it. For those we had these cardboard trays that we'd use for the cakes, so people wouldn't have to take our plates home.

"Look," said Mom, showing me a video.

It showed Uncle Mike building the donut cake. He arranged it just so, then plunged the dowels through. Then Nans did the decorations on top and along the cake tray at the bottom.

"That is so cool," I said.

"Now we have to figure out the hard part," said Mom.

"What's the hard part?" I asked. "The cake is done."

"Yep, the cake is done," said Mom. "And it's sitting

there in the kitchen looking beautiful. And since it's relatively easy to make, and we can use donuts we have stocked, it's a great item to be able to offer from a pricing standpoint."

That's my mom the accountant for you, always thinking of those things.

"But," said Mom, "the hardest part is . . . how the heck do you get a thing like that home?"

I looked at the cake. "Carefully?" I joked.

Mom laughed. "Yes, but we have to find a supplier who has a box large enough and sturdy enough that people can put the cakes in their cars and take them home. The hardest thing about being a baker for special occasions isn't always making the cake. It's about getting it to the party in one piece. The boxes should be here by the end of the week. Then we'll test them out."

"Test out the boxes?"

"Yes," said Mom. "You don't want to box up a cake, hand it to someone, then find out later that it was smashed to smithereens when it slid all over the place on the way home. We'll have to box up a few and drive around and see how they work out."

"A donut test drive!" I said.

"A donut test drive?" asked Dad, setting down a bowl of salad. "Sign me up for that."

Mom and I laughed because Dad had been quiet this whole time, concentrating on making the salad. But of course he heard the words "donut test drive."

"Oops," said Mom. "C'mon, Kels, and help me finish setting the table for this beautiful dinner your dad made."

❊   ❊   ❊   ❊   ❊

After dinner I thought about my blog assignment. I had technically done it at school, but I wondered if Ms. Parkour was right about writing things out making you feel better, so I figured I'd try it.

I found a cool blog template online and played around with it a little bit, changing up the color of the type. I even added a picture of myself at the top, just for fun. I mean, no one was going to see this but me.

I needed a name. Most blogs had names.

How It Feels to Be Me, I typed in.

Nah, that was totally boring. Most blogs had cool names.

The Way Kelsey Sees It (ick)

Kelsey's Korner (maybe?)

Kel-See (really bad)

It's Just Me . . . Kelsey.

I stopped. It was accurate. And the blog was about how I felt. I kind of liked it.

It felt right, so I started to type.

I feel like a big sigh. I feel like nothing's wrong but nothing is right, either. I feel like I'm waiting for something, but I don't know what.

Tonight, I found out that my idea for a donut cake might actually happen, which should be exciting. If it happens. I didn't realize there was so much that goes into thinking about a little cake.

Like, who thinks about how strong a box is when you're making a delicious cake?

Sometimes you have these great ideas, like balloons that go floating by. Pretty, right? But then someone pokes the balloon and it pops and you think maybe the idea wasn't so great anymore.

And also, this is just a little cake we're

talking about. I didn't answer an important question like to how to live on the moon or anything.

My mom always likes to say it's about perspective, which is how you see things, or how you frame them.

My perspective is that the good and the bad just usually average each other out and you land in the middle. Is the middle bad, though? If it's not too bad and not too good? It's just . . .

I sighed.

That was it: I still felt like one big sigh.

Chapter Seven
Keep on Rolling

The rest of the week went pretty fast. The weather wasn't great, but at least the rain cleared out. It was just gray and chilly, like the weather was waiting to either go back to cold rain or slide into warm sun, and it couldn't decide which way to go.

When I walked into the Park on Friday to start my shift, Lindsay was practically hopping up and down behind the counter.

"It's Box Day!" she squealed.

"Okay," I said. "Um . . . are you excited about boxes?"

"Yes!" she said. "Because my dad and Nans made the donut cakes. The boxes are here, so we're all going to take one home and see how it goes."

"Cool!" I said, starting to get excited too. "I'm going to take a peek!"

I ran back to the kitchen and waited at the door.

Have you ever noticed that most kitchen doors in restaurants have little windows in them? It's because there are usually waiters and waitresses going in and out in a hurry, sometimes with big trays of food. The last thing you want to do is smash a door into someone carrying someone else's dinner.

It's happened before. And I don't even need to tell you how Grandpa feels about it.

I peeked through the door and then pushed it open.

There were big counters along the side of the kitchen that were reserved for Nans's desserts and Uncle Mike's donuts. There were sometimes big trays straight from the oven loaded with treats, and I learned the hard way that you can't just grab something off them without getting yelled at.

First of all, everything in a restaurant, as Mom will tell you, is carefully calculated. So for instance, Nans knows, when she makes a batch of cookies, how many baked cookies should come out of the oven. Grandpa and Nans then take the cost of the ingredients and divide that by the number of finished cookies and figure out the price per cookie.

Mom taught me all this, which we call "cookie math." If Nans burns a batch or the waitstaff drops a tray (that actually happens a lot) or the batter ends up making fewer cookies, you could be losing money.

And if a kid like me comes in and starts eating the cookies, that throws off the equation.

Nans is a lot less strict than anyone else and almost always gives her grandchildren cookies anyway. She will also take a plate of cookies to give away for free to customers she knows or ones who have kids.

When I asked Mom about this, she said, "There's always a cost of doing business."

I don't know exactly what she meant by that, but I think it means you don't mess with Nans, especially about cookies.

The counter held six donut-tower cakes. Each had a name card in front: *Grandpa/Nans*, *Charlie*, *Mike*, *Melissa*, *Volunteer #1*, and *Volunteer #2*. Melissa was Mom.

"Hi, sweetie!" said Mom, who was snapping pictures.

"Hi!" I said. "So it's Donut Test Drive Day?"

"Sure is!" said Mom. "We're going to have ourselves an adventurous drive home tonight!"

"Who are Volunteers number one and two?" I asked.

"We felt like we needed at least six people to participate so we'd get some reliable results," said Mom. "So hopefully some of our brave waitstaff, cooks, or kitchen staff will volunteer."

"Maybe not Lily," I whispered.

My cousin Lily was a terrible driver. Like absolutely horrible.

We had a slight problem because in one week she had two accidents in the parking lot, and that meant two customers who were not very happy. Uncle Charlie usually drives her to work now.

Mom stifled a laugh. "That's not nice!" she said. "But actually, maybe she'd be a good test case!"

I headed back out to the counter feeling kind of good for the first time in a while. Nothing major had happened to make my mood change. I wasn't wildly excited, but I wasn't feeling too icky, either.

I still felt like I was in the middle, but . . . this time the middle felt better.

I bounded over to the counter.

"We each get to take home one of those cakes!" I said to Lindsay.

"I know." Lindsay smiled. "Skylar is going to absolutely lose his mind when we come walking in the door with ours."

"I think Molly and Jenna will be pretty psyched too," I said.

"But Molly especially," Lindsay said, and we both laughed.

We have always joked that Molly couldn't work at Donut Dreams because she loves, loves, loves donuts, and she'd eat an entire tray each shift she worked. And as her sister, I can assure you that Molly could totally finish off two dozen donuts easily. That's why she usually works the floor instead.

We each had one "off week" a month during the school year, so we'd have a little break. This was Molly's week off.

Our shift was pretty busy. A lot of parents come in after school for donuts (lucky kids), or they buy them on their way home to bring into their offices or activities in the morning.

The East twins come in one day a week after school with their mom. When they do, Lindsay and I both cringe because it's usually on a Friday, which is when we're working.

They're sweet boys, but holy moly, can those two boys make a total mess. You'd think that eating donuts couldn't be that disastrous, but if you thought that, you haven't seen the grossness of the East twins eating.

"Batten down the hatches," Lindsay said. "The winds are blowing in from the East."

It's kind of funny that Lindsay has a code for when they come in since, with the counter at the front of the Park, I can totally see who is coming as well as she can, but I go along with it.

"Aye, aye, Captain," I said. "Hatches are battening!"

The boys bounded in yelling, "Donut Day! It's Donut Day!"

And as usual, their mother was behind them by a few steps, with a ton of stuff falling out of her bag. Today, her car keys were hanging from her sunglasses. Which were on her head.

I wondered if I should mention that.

"Hey, guys!" I said cheerily.

They were messy, but they were really cute kids.

"Hi, Kelsey! Hi, Lindsay!" they said.

"We have a new flavor," I said. "I think you might like it. It's called Sprinkle Surprise!"

Lindsay kicked me in the shin.

I shrugged. They were going to make a mess even if they ate a plain donut.

"What's a Sprinkle Surprise?" asked Jason.

"It's a donut filled with sprinkles inside and on top!" I said. "See?" I pointed to them in the case.

Jason squatted down, putting his hands on the front of the case, which made me flinch, since I knew we'd have to clean it.

"You just told us and ruined the surprise!" said Jason.

"She didn't say they were in every donut," said Lindsay, saving me. "So it's a surprise if they're in yours or not!"

Jason's twin brother, Christopher, bent down next to him, and said, "Yum!"

Then he . . . licked the case.

"Oh my goodness, Christopher!" yelped Mrs. East. "We do not lick things! Especially glass!"

Lindsay looked like she might gag.

"It's okay," I said, grabbing my squirt bottle and a cloth and running around the front.

"Here," I said to Jason. "Squirt this."

He looked at me and grinned, then squirted the bottle very carefully exactly at the spot Christopher had licked.

"Great helper!" I said.

"Now me!" yelled Christopher.

"You are the wiper," I said, handing him the cloth.

He took it and swiped enthusiastically from one end of the case to the other. There were now long, foggy streak marks across the entire case.

"We can fix that later," I said.

"I'm so sorry," said Mrs. East. "I can clean that off for you."

"No, no," I said. "It's okay!"

"What can we get you today?" asked Lindsay.

I knew we were both thinking the same thing: *Let's get them out of here . . . fast.*

"I want a Sprinkle Surprise!" yelled Christopher. Then he looked up at me. "Very please."

I laughed. "Very please? Sure then, because you have wonderful manners."

"Licking the case is not good manners!" said Jason. "I would like a Sprinkle Surprise too, very please. And I would like one with a lot more sprinkles than the one Christopher gets, very very please."

"We take sprinkles very seriously," said Lindsay. "We measure them so we make sure each donut has the exact same amount."

I almost laughed, but I bit my lip.

"I thought you said it was a surprise if there were sprinkles in it!" Jason said.

"Yes, it's a surprise that there are sprinkles inside," I said, trying to cover. Then I leaned down and whispered, "But you boys are in on the secret."

"We can keep a secret," said Jason.

"Okay, we'll take two Sprinkle Surprise donuts, one jelly for me, and one for my husband, please," said Mrs. East. "He likes the cream-filled."

"For here or to go?" asked Lindsay, and I knew we were both holding our breath.

"Oh, to go today, please," said Mrs. East. "With no rain, we're headed across to the playground to get these kids some fresh air."

"Oh, that's a great, totally wonderful, perfect idea," said Lindsay, and I bit my lip so hard to keep from laughing that I think it started to bleed a little bit.

She rang up Mrs. East while I packed the bag. I handed Mrs. East a stack of napkins.

"Just in case you might need some extras," I said.

After they left, I peered out the window and sighed as I noticed Mrs. East searching in her bag for her keys. Then she put her hand on her head and located them.

"I'm kind of glad I'm not allowed to babysit yet," I said to Lindsay.

"Can you imagine babysitting them?" she yelped. "No way."

I squirted the case again, this time getting all the grime off.

"Clear as a bell!" said Grandpa as he came up behind me.

"Did you see what those kids just did?" I asked. "One of them licked the case!"

"I've seen worse," said Grandpa, shrugging. He looked at his watch. "Okay, in five minutes we close the counter. Clear it on out!"

Then he spun around and went back to patrolling the floor. Grandpa had an eagle eye for detail at the restaurant. He saw every crooked fork on a table, every crumb that dropped, even extra salt flakes on a chair. There was absolutely nothing he missed.

At the end of the shift, Lindsay and I have to

clean the counter, wipe down the shelves inside the case, and do the inventory, which means we type the number of donuts we've sold into a tablet and enter the number we have left over. Then we take the extra donuts back into the kitchen, where we pack them up so they can be donated.

After the restaurant closes, Grandpa drives boxes of donuts around town to fire stations, the police station, and the senior center.

On the way back to the kitchen, we turned off the neon DONUT DREAMS sign and placed a CLOSED FOR NOW, OPEN TOMORROW MORNING! sign on the counter.

We carried the trays into the kitchen and packed up the boxes. Then we took out the garbage and hosed off the trash can.

Once we were done, we took off our aprons. I pulled out my ponytail and shook out my hair.

"Are the contestants ready for the Donut Test Drive?" announced Uncle Mike in his best announcer voice. "Will the participant Melissa please come to the podium to accept her challenge?"

Mom walked over to the table and held up her hand, pretending that it was a microphone. "I would like to say that I'm going to get the trophy in this challenge. I have fantastic driving skills and a family who can take down this cake in about three seconds."

"Do I detect some bravado?" Uncle Charlie asked. "I would like to say that the boxes I ordered are the finest, highest quality. They will assure safe delivery!"

"Even if Lily is driving?" asked Uncle Mike.

"Mike!" said Nans, who was laughing.

"All right, contestants," said Uncle Mike, back in his announcer voice. "Let the games begin!"

He lifted up the cakes while Nans slid the boxes underneath them. Then he carefully lowered them in, and Nans closed the lids. They tied twine around each box to hold it together.

Everyone waited a second.

"Okay, we're going to have to see if this works," said Mom.

She went to pick up the box, and Uncle Mike and Nans yelled, "From the bottom!" at the same time.

Mom rolled her eyes and picked up the box from the bottom.

"Get my keys, Kels," she said.

I fished them out of her bag. I held open the back door to the kitchen, and Mom carefully walked down the steps. I opened the trunk and she slid the box in.

Ready to Roll!

When the trunk was halfway down, I yelled, "Watch it!" as the box almost got crushed. We slid the cake in farther, and then Mom firmly shut the trunk, peering inside.

Uncle Mike, Lindsay, Uncle Charlie, and Nans were watching from the top step. Uncle Mike slapped his head as he watched, and Uncle Charlie yelled, "Way to look out from the start, Liss!"

Mom shook her head and started the car. She backed out slowly, rolled out of the parking lot, and we were on our way.

"We're rolling!" she said.

"Whatever you do, Mom," I said, "keep rolling and don't stop short."

Chapter Eight
Ready to Roll

The good news was that we got the cake home in one piece. Mom drove a little more slowly than usual, and aside from one very sharp turn that made the box slide across the back of the car, we had an uneventful trip.

Mom walked in the door, proudly holding the enormous cake box, and Molly, Jenna, and Dad crowded around.

I held my breath as we cut the twine and lifted the lid off.

"Oh my," said Dad. "That is spectacular."

"Can we just have that for dinner?" asked Molly.

Mom and Dad shot her looks.

"Never hurts to ask," she said.

"Now the issue is," said Mom, "how do we get this thing out?"

She stood on her tiptoes, but she couldn't reach down deep enough into the box to lift the tray.

"I think I can reach," said Dad.

"That's not the issue," said Mom. "We can't have a height requirement for getting these out."

"Can you cut the box open?" asked Jenna.

"Good idea," said Mom, and she got the scissors. "But which way?"

All of us had ideas. Mom was getting frustrated, so finally she started at the top and then just cut a straight line down the center.

"All that did was split it open," I said. "We have to do it wider to get the cake out."

"Do the same thing on the back side," said Dad.

Mom did, and then they carefully folded down the two halves, revealing the cake.

Mom lifted it out and peered at it. "Okay, no crushing or smearing. Well, a little smear here but nothing catastrophic."

"But getting it out of the box is kind of a problem," I said.

Mom nodded. "Major problem. We'll see what

the others in the test group come back with," she said. "Now dinner first. Then we do the taste test."

It was Jenna's turn to set the table, so I went upstairs and flopped down on my bed. I opened my laptop and opened *It's Just Me . . . Kelsey.*

When you are in a blah state, sometimes small or dumb things make you happy in weird ways.

Today, I was happy that we got a cake in a box. Which, I mean, it's a cake. In a box. It's not important. Maybe I was just happy to be around my family. Maybe I'm excited that an idea I had could actually work as a business, which would be pretty cool.

But then I was disappointed because we had trouble getting the cake out of the box, which means maybe it won't work out after all. When you swing up and then you swing back down, you land in the middle.

Which is sometimes okay and sometimes, just blah.

"Dinnertime!" Mom called upstairs.

Ready to Roll!

Mom has a thing that when she calls you for dinner, you need to be at the table in about three minutes. Even if you're in the middle of a homework assignment, or if you're in the middle of a shower, or if you were in a spaceship headed to Mars, it doesn't matter.

When dinner is ready, it's like everything stops, and you need to beam yourself into your assigned chair.

And, yes, it is really annoying.

I went downstairs quickly because I didn't feel like getting barked at by anyone besides Rusty. Dad had made meatballs and spaghetti, which usually made me happy.

"Cold night, warm dinner," he said, placing the bowls on the table.

"Perfect," said Mom.

"Oh, not much is ever perfect," said Dad.

"I'll say," I said, biting into a piece of bread.

Mom and Dad exchanged looks but didn't grill me.

"Best and worst thing," said Mom.

Every night at dinner we do a "best and worst," where we each have to state the best thing and the worst thing that happened that day.

Jenna's best was always that she got an A on a test

or she won some sort of award. She was like Super Sister.

Her worst thing was generally that she didn't break a record doing something. Or that she was worried that her fifteen activities weren't enough to get her into her first-choice college.

Molly's best usually involved soccer.

"Kelsey, you're up first."

I stuffed my mouth with a forkful of pasta and motioned to Molly.

"Okay," said Mom. "Molly?"

"Soccer is starting again, so that's the best thing," said Molly.

She was always pretty predictable.

"Worst is that you should see this new training schedule. It's brutal. The number of drills that I need to do is insane, and if it doesn't stop raining, I'm going to have to do them inside."

"No, no, no," said Mom and Dad at once.

"No more soccer incidents!" said Dad. "I'm still fixing things from the last soccer season."

Last season Molly took out a window and a baseboard, and dented a wall with a soccer ball.

"Jen, how about you?" asked Mom.

"Best thing is that my schedule at the Park is light this week," said Jenna. "Which means I can get ahead on my paper that's due. Which is also the worst thing, since the paper is on the history of how women are treated in the workplace and it's really depressing."

"Well," said Mom. "It's also important for you to see how far women have come, so that your generation can be part of the movement toward equality."

Jenna and Mom talked for what seemed like an hour about how women were taken for granted and not paid as much as men and were put at a disadvantage if they chose to have kids and work, which was unfair.

I mean, I knew it was important stuff, and definitely affected me or at least my future self. But I was just . . . blah.

I guess I had totally tuned them out, because when I looked up, they were all looking at me.

"What?" I asked.

"What was the best and worst thing today?" asked Mom.

"Oh, that," I said. "The best was seeing those cakes, because that's kind of cool. The worst . . ." I stopped. "I guess the worst is that now that the delivery system doesn't work, we might not be able to do it. It just seems like so much is back and forth, like good, then bad. And I keep landing up in this blah middle. I mean, it's just a stack of donuts that was done for fun, and now it's this big deal."

Mom looked at me with that worried look she gets.

"It's a box, drama queen," said Jenna.

"Jenna!" said Dad sharply. "It's about a little more than the box."

"Yeah," said Jenna. "But I mean, they can figure that out. It's not like 'oh, all my hopes and dreams are lost because of a box!'"

I scowled at her. "But true importance is a tennis match, right, Jenna?"

Jenna scowled back at me.

"Okay," said Mom. "Time-out here. We need to be respectful and listen to each other. That's what this is all about. I think what Kelsey is saying is that she's in a bit of a funk and a little overwhelmed that a simple idea is snowballing into a bigger venture."

I thought for a second.

"Yeah, I guess that's it," I said slowly.

Mom and Dad had one of those secret communication looks. Like you can tell they're talking to each other without saying anything.

They gave each other one before Dad said, "Sometimes being stuck with things just 'okay' is good. It means there's nothing terribly wrong, and that's a good thing. Sometimes that's reassuring, and sometimes it's frustrating."

I nodded.

"And you're right," said Mom. "There's still a long way to go in launching a donut cake business. We have a long way before we're ready to roll. But we're talking about it and working through the challenges. These things just take time, so you have to hang in there."

We all finished dinner quietly.

After dinner Mom and Dad made a fire in the fireplace. Jenna made some popcorn, and we all dragged blankets and pillows in and piled on the floor of the family room, close to the warmth of the fire, listening to the crackle.

Rusty nuzzled in between Jenna and me, putting his head on my back.

"Mmmmm," said Molly. "This feels good."

"I'm in a donut haze," said Dad.

We had taken apart the donut cake, as Mom

predicted, in about three seconds flat. It was good, but to be honest, it didn't really taste that different from just eating a donut.

Don't get me wrong, the donuts were delicious, as usual, but as Mom said, "This is all about the presentation."

"Plus," said Molly, "donuts are still a treat. I mean, we look at this as 'oh, these taste like the same donuts we always get,' but most people don't have the direct access to donuts on a daily basis that we do."

"Great point," said Mom.

Now Mom was flipping through her phone. "Hey," she said, holding it up. "Kelsey, did you send me these photos?"

I squinted over, then nodded. They were of the first donut cake I made. When I sent them out to everyone, I had styled them with some text bursts and drew some flowers over them using this app I have on my phone.

"This is it," said Mom, sitting up.

We all looked up, and she gave me a look I've seen before. It meant, *I'm not messing around.*

"Kelsey," she said. "You and I are going to make this work. We are on a roll."

Chapter Nine
Kelsey's Kakes

I would never underestimate Mom. Anytime, anywhere. When she says something is going to happen, it does. And there is simply no changing her mind. I've been on that side of it, and trust me, once Mom says, "This is it," you should just get out of the way and accept it.

By Monday night she had whipped up a business plan for the donut cakes that included a marketing plan.

I had never heard of a marketing plan before, but according to Mom, it was "essential" for any business, and it basically covered how you would let people know about your services so they'd want to order a cake.

We were sitting in her office and she was flipping through pages on her computer with a ton of numbers that showed what the marketing budget was, how many cakes they'd need to sell, and how much everything would cost, from the dowels to the donuts to the boxes and even the twine to wrap them.

There were so many numbers and so many details, it was giving me a headache.

I just kind of nodded because I had no idea what any of this had to do with me, until she said, "And here's where we need you."

She turned to a page that had a sign: *Kelsey's Kakes.*

I looked at it, then at her.

"What's that?" I asked, a bit nervous.

Mom smiled. "That's what Grandpa wants to call the donut cake business."

"Kelsey's Kakes?" I said, and my stomach did a little flutter. "He knows that's not how you spell 'cakes,' right?"

Mom laughed. "Yes, he's actually quite a good speller. But you know that while he loves all his grandchildren, he has a soft spot for you. And since this was your idea, he feels it should be named after you. Kind of an honor, don't you think?"

I thought about it for a minute. On one hand, that was pretty cool. On the other . . . Molly was not going to like it. And maybe I didn't either.

"Aren't other people, like other people who might be my sister, going to be a little hurt?"

Mom shrugged. "They may give us a bit of flak for that, but I don't think anyone is going to be mortally offended here. It *was* your idea."

"I sense Molly's Muffins might be coming soon," I said.

"Actually," Mom said, "that's not a bad idea. And if Molly presents that, then she'll get something named after her too."

Mom looked at me. "This is yours. And we're all going to help get it off the ground. Why are you hesitating?"

I sighed and shrugged. Now my stomach and my heart were fluttering a little bit.

"Here's where we need you to come in," said Mom. "I showed everyone those photos you took and then styled with the drawn hearts and the speech balloons. It's a cool look. So we're thinking of adding a link on our web page to Kelsey's Kakes. The Kelsey's Kakes site will be styled with these elements. We'll also make sure the logo and everything attached to Kelsey's Kakes is consistent."

Everything attached to Kelsey's Kakes?

My heart wasn't just fluttering. It was starting to race.

Then Mom flipped to the next page. "This"—she pointed—"is where we need you."

That's when I saw a big picture of me smiling, with some blank space under it.

"Mom," I said, feeling tense. "What is that?"

"I think you could have a small blog on the Kelsey's Kakes page talking about the cakes, what we offer, and how to order them, but do it in your voice."

"So I'm the voice of Kelsey's Kakes?"

"You are the face and the voice of Kelsey's Kakes," said Mom proudly.

I started biting my nails, which I only ever do when I get really stressed out about something.

"What's wrong?" asked Mom.

"It's just . . . a lot," I said. "And can we not put my face on the website? That's kind of freaking me out."

Mom nodded in understanding. "Sure, I get that. Maybe we can just use a drawing of you instead."

"Or nothing," I said. "Just the logo."

"Okay," said Mom, watching me. "Talk to me. What else?"

"How much will I have to write here?"

"Truthfully, we'll write a lot of it with you, especially talking about the pricing and the ordering process. The rest is up to you. You really don't need to post more than once a week."

I felt itchy for some reason.

"Okay, this is a lot," said Mom. "We're going to work on the financial side, which still needs to be worked out before we roll this out. You think about it. We have some time before we'll need to finalize anything, and if you aren't comfortable, we're not going to force anything on you."

"Even the name?" I asked.

"That," Mom said, "Grandpa is really set on. But of course if it makes you unhappy, we can rename it."

"Okay," I said.

I headed upstairs, feeling glad that at least Mom said nothing was finalized.

Until I remembered one thing: the only person more difficult to change once they set their minds on something was Grandpa.

❉   ❉   ❉   ❉   ❉

Dad's advice when I was a little unsure about something new was to think it through as if it was already happening.

I'd been really nervous about the first day of middle school, so Dad and I had this game over the summer where he played "act as if." So he'd have me run through what I thought would happen the first day, good or bad.

Then we'd talk about what would happen if any of those things actually came true (like, for instance, if I got lost in the hall between classes or if I had no one to sit with at lunch).

So I decided to act "as if."

I opened my laptop and pulled up *It's Just Me . . . Kelsey* and copied the template. Then I typed in *Kelsey's Kakes* at the top.

Who wants a tower of happiness for their next celebration? You can order a big stack of happy donut cakes at Kelsey's Kakes!

I paused. What else could I say? It was a stack of

donuts. There wasn't much more to it.

I flipped back to my *It's Just Me . . .* blog.

Sometimes things are really simple and make you happy. There's not more to them, and that's okay, because being happy, even just for a second, is good.

But what happens when people think you have to make it bigger than it is? What happens when a little happiness starts rolling into a big production?

That makes me feel overwhelmed. And like I'm going to have to take a big breath in and out. Which I guess is still feeling like a big sigh.

Again.

I shut my laptop. Maybe I was worried about nothing. After all, there were a lot of kids who would like a whole business named after them.

And I was pretty sure one of them was sleeping across the hall from me.

Chapter Ten
Donut Trouble

By the time I opened the door to the Park on Friday for my shift at Donut Dreams, I was a big bag of nerves.

Mom had revealed that Grandpa wanted to name the new business Kelsey's Kakes and, as expected, Molly was pretty mad.

Mom had told us casually that morning while we were eating breakfast, which maybe wasn't the greatest timing.

Dad has to leave early in the morning to get to the high school to teach, so Mom is in charge of getting us all up and out the door. And just in case you're wondering what it's like to be herded in the morning by a very organized, detail-oriented person, Dad's nickname for Mom in the morning is the General.

Mom sets the table for breakfast the night before and wakes us up at precisely the same time every day. When we were younger, there was actually a checklist next to the back door listing everything we were supposed to do before we left, like make our bed, brush our teeth, make sure we had our lunches and backpacks.

We had to put a check mark next to every item. Mom would then make sure there were checks next to everything before she drove us to school.

When we come downstairs at seven o'clock every morning, Mom is always showered, dressed for work, and has all our lunches out and ready on the counter.

She eats her breakfast at the Park, but she always makes coffee and is walking around with the biggest mug I've ever seen.

So Friday morning, Molly and I were eating and Jenna, as usual, was still upstairs fussing over her hair.

Mom was calling, "Down in five, Jenna, and I'm not kidding!" which usually made Jenna even crankier, and she started out cranky on a good morning.

Jenna finally came down the stairs and grabbed her yogurt from the fridge.

Mom and Dad were very strict that we had to eat breakfast in the morning, and it had to be healthy. I was totally jealous that my friend Hannah was allowed to eat donuts or sugary cereal.

The three of us were quietly eating when Mom said, "So you're probably as excited as I am about this new donut cake business."

"Probably not," said Molly.

Jenna giggled. "It's a cool idea, Mom."

"It was your sister's idea," said Mom, "and it's really rolling along. It looks like we're going to be able to launch Kelsey's Kakes in a few weeks."

"That's great, Mom," mumbled Jenna.

"If they're Kelsey's cakes, does she get to eat them all?" joked Molly.

"They'll be called Kelsey's Kakes, with 'kakes' spelled with a *K*, because Kelsey came up with the idea," said Mom.

"Wait, there's going to be a line of cakes called Kelsey's Kakes?" asked Jenna.

"That's the plan," said Mom.

Jenna and Molly looked at me.

"It was Grandpa's idea," I said nervously.

"Yes, that's right," said Mom. "Grandpa likes the

idea of naming them after Kelsey because she thought of the idea. We'll be launching a separate website with her name on it, and we're hopeful that this might turn into a really good business for us."

"She's going to have her own website?" asked Jenna.

"It will be linked to the Park," said Mom, "but yes."

"That will look good for her college applications," said Jenna. She seriously had a one-track mind.

"Wait, wait, wait," said Molly. "I mean, I know Kelsey is Grandpa's favorite, but everyone is all about being equal and equally special and loved, so how come she gets something named after her and none of us do? Not even Donut Dreams is named after someone!"

You could kind of tell Mom had been waiting for this.

"Kelsey is not Grandpa's favorite. He loves all his grandchildren equally. But this was her idea. Donut Dreams was Nans's idea, and she chose that name herself."

Molly glared at me and rolled her eyes.

"Grandpa totally has favorites."

"How about 'Hey, that's really cool, Kelsey!'" said Mom.

"That's cool, Kelsey," Jenna repeated in a monotone.

Molly refused to look at me.

Mom sighed. "I think it's fantastic."

She glanced at the clock. "Okay, crew, let's head out. Last day before the weekend . . ."

She grabbed her keys from the hook next to the door where she always kept them and watched while we loaded our dishes into the dishwasher, grabbed our lunches, and filed out the door.

Molly and I don't see too much of each other during the day, but when I passed her in the halls, she didn't really seem to react. Maybe she was just annoyed but not really angry.

When I opened the door to the Park later in the afternoon, I was ready for the possibility that Lindsay was going to be at least as annoyed as Molly.

I had done the "act as if" game Dad had taught me and was running through everything I could say to Lindsay if she was as peeved as Molly.

First, I went into the kitchen and said hello to Nans.

"Saved a Sprinkle Surprise for you," she said,

84

nodding toward a plate with a donut on it and a glass of milk set out next to it.

"Thanks, Nans," I said. "Is there one for Lindsay, too?"

"Of course," said Nans, pointing behind her, where Lindsay was already sitting with her own donut.

"Oh, I didn't see you, Linds," I said.

She waved, and I sat down next to her.

"How is your new Kelsey's Kakes going?" she asked, her mouth half-full of donut.

"Okay," I said quietly.

"What's the issue?" asked Nans, frosting donuts.

Nans was just like Mom. She had what Grandpa called a "radar for feelings." She could tell if you were happy or sad or upset just by watching you.

Nans worked really quickly, swirling glaze on top, then dipping the donuts in sprinkles before the glaze dried.

"Oh, nothing," I said.

She looked at me.

"Honestly," I said, "I think it's weird that it's called Kelsey's Kakes."

"Why is it weird?" asked Lindsay. "It was your idea."

So much for Lindsay being angry, I thought. *That's at least a win.*

"Yeah," I said. "I mean it was my idea to stack up some donuts so they looked like a cake. That's not really original. It was Uncle Mike and Mom who decided it could be a business."

"So you want it to be called Mike and Melissa's Cakes instead?" asked Lindsay.

"Maybe," I said. "It has a ring to it."

"Kelsey," said Nans. "Grandpa is very proud of this. He sees something in this business, and he's tickled that it started with one of his grandchildren. It's a real honor to have something named after you."

"I know," I said, and I did. But still.

"Shift starts in five," said Lindsay, hopping down from her stool. "I'll meet you out there."

"I'm coming," I said, before I turned to Nans. "How come Donut Dreams isn't named after you?"

"It is!" she said. "That was my little dream business so I could earn enough money to be able to send my kids to college. I chose that name."

Maybe I could come up with a name like Donut Dreams, one that didn't include *my* name.

"Plus," said Nans, "I did have a reason for choosing

Donut Dreams as a name. I wanted to dream that someday one of my children could work at the business too."

"All your children work at the Park!" I said.

"They do," she said. "But Donut Dreams is run by Mike. Donut Dreams was set up so we could send Mike to school out of state if he chose. And the dream was that maybe this business was set up for him to come back to, too."

"So Kelsey's Kakes . . . would be mine?" I asked.

"There's a long way to go," said Nans. "All sorts of things have to happen first, like launching it, for instance. But let's just say if it's successful, and it has a long life and you decide you want to come back and live in Bellgrove and run it, then it's here for you. The Park is here for all of you kids. That's what a family business is for."

That was a lot to think about. How did something that started off as a stack of donuts build into something so complicated?

As I tied my apron behind my back, I thought of one more tough thing: it was Friday. The East twins were about to blow through the door.

Chapter Eleven
Blogs and Jobs

On Monday, Ms. Parkour wanted to check in on our blogs.

"So let's talk about how this process is going," she said. "Are you feeling like your writing is loosening up and getting a little easier, or are any of you struggling?"

Hannah raised her hand.

"I'm finding that all my entries are kind of the same," she said after Ms. Parkour called on her. "I guess maybe I'm not an interesting person, because I kind of feel the same on most days."

"Great point," said Ms. Parkour. "We've been doing this for two weeks, so let's think about it. Unless you have a dramatic thing happen in your life, your feelings or state of mind probably aren't going to change that dramatically, right?"

Everyone shook their heads.

"But I'd like you to peel back under the day-to-day feelings. Let's talk, for instance, about a typical day. Can anyone volunteer a summary of their journaling? Or would anyone like to read snippets to us?"

No one raised their hand as Ms. Parkour scanned the room.

"Let's do this another way, then," she said. "Anyone want to throw out the one word that comes up most often in your blog?"

"Bored!" said Eric, and everyone laughed.

"I'll take it," said Ms. Parkour. "So, Eric, on most days you're bored?"

"Uh," said Eric, "maybe? But not in this class." Everyone laughed again.

Ms. Parkour laughed too. "Oh, of course not in this class, I definitely know that. But let's talk about why you're bored. Is it because there's a monotony about this time of year at school? Is it because, for instance, the next school break is still weeks away? Is it because you're sick of the hazy weather?"

"All of that?" said Eric.

"Okay," said Ms. Parkour. "That's great."

"It's great that I'm bored?" said Eric.

"No," said Ms. Parkour. "But your honesty here is important. So if you're bored with the schedule at school, about the fact that there's no vacation in sight soon, or about the fact that you've been stuck inside, that's all important. And I'd like you to explore those feelings a little deeper in your writing this week. In addition to summing things up in one word, I'd like you to ask yourself *why* you feel that way."

She glanced at the clock. "Okay, we have a few minutes left, so let's start writing."

I took out my laptop and opened it to *It's Just Me . . . Kelsey.*

I still feel up and down. And I guess the definition of up and down without being steady is confused.

Why am I confused? I'm confused because I should be happy about launching a new business, but I'm too worried that everyone's feelings will be hurt because it's named after me.

Molly can be a pain, but she's still my sister. I don't want to hurt her feelings.

And I'm excited about it, but what if it doesn't work? I think it will be cool to be known for Kelsey's Kakes, but what happens if it fails? Will people blame me? Will it be my fault since it's my idea?

So besides confused, now I also feel . . . worried.

The bell rang and I was relieved. The last period was math, and I was grateful to have some work ahead where I could solve problems that had definitive answers.

It was no surprise that it was raining again by last period.

I was glad to have Dad picking me up, and today, it was just me because Molly was staying after school for soccer training.

Dad flicked the lights, and I couldn't help grinning as I walked quickly to the car and slid in as fast as I could.

"Hello, love," said Dad. "Funny how we keep meeting up like this!"

I laughed. "Dad, you're so corny. Thanks for picking me up."

"Oh, it's my pleasure," he said. "And it's just you and me today. Jenna is staying after school for a student council meeting, and Molly will be at practice until five o'clock."

You'd think with three kids we didn't get a lot of alone time with our parents, but they did a pretty good job of figuring out how to have some "one-on-one" time, as they called it, with each of us.

"I actually have to finish up a project in my shed," said Dad.

Dad teaches woodworking, but he's a carpenter on the weekends and during the summer. He works on all different kinds of projects, from building bookcases in offices to working on the construction of a house.

"How about you bring your snack out there and keep me company?"

"Deal," I said.

I loved Dad's shed. It always smelled of sawdust, even though he kept it really neat. He had all his tools precisely organized.

We grabbed some bananas, graham crackers, and

peanut butter and ran from the house to the shed, which was in the far corner of the backyard.

I sat at a counter Dad had built and he put on his safety goggles.

He had to measure out and cut some pieces of plywood for a project, and he had all these tools ready to make sure that everything was measured correctly. Dad wasn't as precise as Mom usually, but he was when it came to woodworking.

I watched him for a while as I ate my snack. I knew when he was measuring he didn't like to be interrupted.

I sliced the banana and then stacked it up, putting layers of peanut butter in between and sprinkling raisins around it.

He cut two rectangles, then stood back, measured them again, and took off his safety goggles.

"Hard part is done," said Dad. "I just have to sand these and stain them now."

He glanced over.

"Hey, you built something too!" he said, grinning.

"Want some?" I asked.

Dad took a piece of banana and licked his finger. "You really have a talent there."

"For stacking food?" I said.

"Well," said Dad, "there's a little more to it than stacking food. You have an artistic eye."

"I may have an artistic eye for stacking donuts," I said. "But that doesn't really seem like a true talent, Dad."

"Of course it is," said Dad. "Do you know there's actually a career you could pursue as a food stylist?"

"A what?" I asked.

"A food stylist," said Dad. "They're the ones who style food artistically for commercials or advertising shoots. They have all sorts of tricks up their sleeves to make everything look delicious."

"Huh," I said. "That's kind of cool. So you think I should be a food stylist?"

"I'm not saying that," said Dad, "although it's certainly an option. What I'm saying is that everyone sees that you have a real talent, and it will be interesting to see how you develop it into something."

"What if I just like stacking things?" I asked. "Maybe I don't develop it into anything."

"That's okay too!" said Dad. He started sanding the wood. "Here, help me out with this." He handed me a piece of sanding paper.

We sanded together, not talking, going back and forth and making a *scratch, scratch, scratch* noise.

"Do you think it's weird that they want to name the cake business Kelsey's Kakes?" I asked.

"Not at all," said Dad. "Do you?"

"Yeah," I said. "It means I'm the only grandchild who has something named after them."

"True," said Dad. "But this was your idea."

"Everyone keeps saying that!" I said, exasperated. "And yeah, I stacked some donuts up. But Uncle Mike and Mom are the ones who are planning the whole thing out and getting it off the ground. I mean, I didn't even know what a dowel is, and I hadn't considered the box or how to get it home. I'm just a kid who stacked a few donuts."

Dad sanded for a bit more before he answered.

"You've been in a little bit of a blah state," he said.

I nodded.

"And you're surrounded by Lindsay, and Jenna and Molly, even your cousins Rich and Lily, who are all eager to leave our small town. Jenna can't wait to get out to California, and Molly has big plans for a city too."

"Yeah," I said. "And I want to stay here."

I wondered what this had to do with donuts.

"And you want to stay here," said Dad, "which is fine because that's what Mom and I did too. So I think what this is all about . . ."

I waited.

"I think this is about Mom seeing that you're a lot like her."

"Dad, are you serious?" I said. "I'm pretty much nothing like Mom! I'm not overly organized, I don't love numbers, and I have zero interest in being an accountant. Also, I don't run fast. At all."

Dad laughed. "Okay, okay. I said you're like her, but you aren't a replication of her. Mom loves living here. When she went to college, she aced all her classes. She graduated with insanely high grades and was the president of every organization."

"Yep, I've heard those stories," I said. "Grandpa likes to talk about them."

"You also know she was offered jobs in cities," Dad said.

"Uh-huh," I said.

"Big jobs," Dad said. "Impressive jobs with fancy titles. She could have been on her way to very powerful positions."

"But," I said, "she wanted to come home."

"But," Dad said, nodding, "she wanted to come home. And there's nothing wrong with that, and you could even say it worked out pretty well for her. But Grandpa and Nans were not too happy at first."

"What?" I said. "I haven't heard that part before."

"I know," said Dad. "But Grandpa and Nans couldn't understand why Mom would rather come home and work at the Park instead of a big investment firm in Chicago. They thought she was just afraid to try. But she wasn't. She knew what she wanted, and she was perfectly fine with the decision she made. She never looked back."

I started to understand.

"So you mean because I talk about staying here and living here for the rest of my life, Mom wants me to know that's okay?" I asked.

"Yes," said Dad. "She understands that you'll have some pressure to 'do bigger' or 'try something new.' And I think she wants you to know that there's something they're building here that you can come back to, if you'd like."

"Dad, you know I can't start my own company," I said. "I'm in middle school! Maybe she could just have a conversation with me instead of launching a new business."

"Yes, we are all aware that you're only twelve, which is why no one has come out and said that Kelsey's Kakes could be the start of a business for you. For all we know, in the next ten years you'll decide to become an astronaut, and you'll be hurtling into space, which is pretty far from Bellgrove."

"Ugh," I said. "Dad, you know I get nauseous easily. I could never be an astronaut! I once threw up on the teacup ride at the fair."

"I know," said Dad. "I was the one you threw up on."

"Sorry," I said.

"You can make it up to me," he said, taking off his work gloves and putting all his tools back. "You can make it up to me right now by helping me get dinner ready while I go pick up Molly from practice."

"Deal," I said, "but only if you make something I can stack."

Chapter Twelve
Ready to Go Beta!

I now had two blogs to manage, *It's Just Me* . . . and the one for Kelsey's Kakes.

The Kelsey's Kakes blog was fun because I was just writing about party ideas. Mom told me to write like the business was already open, so I was offering party ideas to go with certain donut cakes.

If, for instance, you were having a party with a construction theme for a kid (which Skylar seemed to have for the first four years of his life), the donut cake could be made with orange-tinted donuts, so it looked like a construction cone.

I had an idea for a donut wedding cake with the theme of "They Put a Ring on It" with rings of donuts piled high, and confetti decorating the cake tray. Another cake was for a fairy party theme, and it featured "fairy dust" on it, which was really just powdered sugar that was tinted different colors.

I was kind of having fun with these ideas, showing pictures of parties and designing the pages.

"I see a future web designer," said Uncle Mike, when I showed him the latest version.

I was getting so sick of people constantly coming up with careers for me, but I decided to take it as a compliment.

It's Just Me . . . should have been an easier blog to manage, but since that was really supposed to be about me and my feelings, it was actually harder. Still, I was at it every night. Some nights were easier than others.

I feel like I'm being pulled in a million directions and landing in the middle.

At school my teachers tell me I need to think about high school. My older sister Jenna tells me I need to think about college. Mom's already thinking about where I'll work when I graduate college.

It's like everyone keeps wanting me to think about what's next.

But what about now?

What about just being okay with things as they are, even if they're just "normal" or "okay"?

Is that boring, like Eric says?

I feel torn. I feel confused. I feel like I'm in the middle of something I don't know how to get out of.

☀ ☀ ☀ ☀ ☀

Tuesday afternoon after school, I was debating whether I wanted a snack when my phone dinged with a text from Mom.

> Ready to go to beta tomorrow! We're rolling! Okay.

What was beta?

?

> Beta means a test run of the website

Oh. I shrugged. Then I started to feel a little nauseous inside. So this was happening. It was going, even if it was just a test. It was going to be "out there."

I wandered across the hall to Molly's room and leaned in the doorway. She was sitting on her window seat, her tablet on her lap, as she banged away at her keyboard.

Knowing Molly, she was probably doing homework that wasn't due for another two weeks.

"Can I help you?" she asked, not looking up.

"Are you mad at me?" I asked.

"What did you do?" asked Molly, still not looking up.

"The whole Kelsey's Kakes thing," I said.

"What about it?" she asked, finally looking up at me coolly.

"It's not my fault," I said.

"Okay," she said.

I stood there uncertainly. "Do you want me to tell them they shouldn't do it, if you're mad?"

"I'm not mad," she said. "I'm not particularly thrilled with the name, but if they launch a new cake business, then that's their business."

"So you want me to change the name?" I asked.

"I'm not asking you to change the name," said

Molly, talking to me like I was one of the East twins.

"But you don't like the name," I said.

"What is wrong with you?" she bellowed.

"Nothing!" I yelled back.

"Then stop bothering me about the stupid name!" yelled Molly.

"What is going on up there?" called Mom.

I guess I hadn't heard her come home.

"Nothing!" we both yelled together.

Molly looked at me. "I don't know what you want from me," she said.

"I don't want anything," I said, and stomped back into my room.

I was sad and mad and confused. These dumb donuts were ruining my life.

At dinner Mom talked nonstop about the new website. They had taken my blog posts and designs, and a professional web designer was managing the site for them.

Mom clicked through on her phone to show us all. Dad was really interested, but Molly barely looked at it as she shoveled her lasagna in her mouth, and Jenna kept finding typos, which made me really crazy.

"This is just a soft launch," said Mom. "The site

will have to be managed and designed differently for the final version, so we'll have time to make some changes."

"So not everyone will be able to see it?" I asked, gnawing at my fingernail.

"You can find it on the main site for the Park, and it will have a link, but to be honest, we don't get that much traffic on that site. So people going there on purpose to find it will be able to."

"Mom, no one goes onto the site because everyone in town knows about the Park," said Jenna.

"True," said Mom. "That's why it's not a great site now. It's more of a bookmark or just a quick lookup if someone wants the phone number or to see the menu."

"Or if they live out of town," said Molly.

"No one ever comes to Bellgrove just to visit," said Jenna, rolling her eyes.

Mom's phone flashed with a text.

Normally she was insanely strict about not having phones at the table during meals, especially dinner. She tried to glance at it.

"We're pretty much done here," teased Dad, "so go ahead and check that."

We all stood up to clear the table.

"Ugh!" said Mom. "There's a problem the web designer is having. Kelsey, I'm going to need to use the actual blog template you created."

"Okay," I said. "Uh, how?"

"She's going to walk me through this," said Mom. "Can you go grab your laptop for me?"

I ran upstairs and brought the computer to her.

Two hours later—and I'm serious, it took two hours—Mom called me back down to the kitchen.

She looked exhausted, and actually, I was pretty tired too.

"I have a surprise for you," Mom said. "We finished earlier than expected."

The website for the Park was up on the screen.

Mom grinned. "Click there!" she said, pointing to the tab that said *Kelsey's Kakes*.

I clicked and there it was . . . the blog. I saw the logo and all the cake ideas, neatly arranged as I had written them. Some had hearts or stars next to them, just as I'd designed them.

"You, baby," said Mom, "are live!"

I blinked. *What?*

I'd been tired about thirty seconds ago. But now I knew I wouldn't be able to sleep.

Chapter Thirteen
Queen of Donuts

I had, of course, told Sophia, Michelle, and Riley about everything. On Wednesday morning when I came into school, they did a little cheer for me.

"It's the cake queen!" said Sophia.

"All hail the queen of donuts!" said Riley, giving me a hug.

"What's this all about?" asked Isabella.

"Kelsey is shy about it, but she has a whole business named after her!" said Sophia.

"Look," said Riley, pulling out her phone and going to the Park site. She clicked on the Kelsey's Kakes button.

"Voilà!" she said dramatically.

"Kelsey, you're famous!" Michelle said.

"Whoa!" said Isabella. "It has your picture and everything!"

My picture?

I looked.

No.

No, no, no.

When I gave Mom the template, I forgot to take the photo of myself off it, and I hadn't noticed it last night.

Oh no. Okay, I thought, trying not to panic.

Mom said this was a beta test. There was still time to change things.

And besides, how many people were really going to look at this thing?

By lunchtime, I had my answer.

I don't know if my friends were just really excited for me or if it was true that news spreads fast in a small town, because as of lunchtime, kids were yelling, "Hey, Kelsey Kakes!" and waving as I sat down at the lunch table.

"This is so embarrassing," I said.

I poked at my lunch, not feeling that hungry.

"Why is it embarrassing?" asked Olivia. "It's so cool! I want one of those for my birthday! I think it would be neat to have one of the fairy ones you talk about. But maybe not fairies. Maybe butterflies."

That was actually a good idea, I thought.

"Can we talk about something other than donuts?" I asked. "Please?"

Sophia put her arm around me.

"Let's talk about whatever you want," she said.

Michelle nodded. "Agreed. Donuts are a no-no."

I smiled.

"Oh, let's talk about the next student council meeting," said Hannah.

I was relieved when she started to talk about voting on something. I wasn't really paying attention to her, but I was grateful to just nod along, picking at my tuna sandwich, and not have to say one thing about donuts.

I was thinking we'd get through lunch when Eric walked over. Eric wasn't a bad kid, but he was so annoying.

"Hey, Kelsey," he said. "I totally get how you feel."

We all stopped talking and looked up at him.

"How I feel?" I asked.

"Yeah," said Eric. "About being bored or stuck or blah. I really relate to that."

I blinked in confusion.

"Oh, I read your blog on Kelsey's Kakes," Eric explained.

"But my blog is about cake and party ideas," I said.

"Yeah, the cake part," said Eric. "I'm taking about your other blog."

I felt every cell in my body get tingly cold, then kind of do a little jiggly shake.

"What?" I said.

"Yeah, the *It's Just Me . . . Kelsey* blog," said Eric.

Sophia opened her tablet and went to the site. "There's just stuff about . . . oh. Wait."

She turned the laptop around so I could see it, and there it was: my blog.

"If you click this," said Sophia, "then it takes you there. It kind of looks like it's a blog behind a blog. Like one was set up, then the other one layered over it."

Of course that was exactly what I'd done. I just didn't think when I gave Mom one that I would accidentally give her both.

"I think . . . ," I said, as my stomach turned over. "I think I'm going to throw up."

And then I just ran to the bathroom.

Two minutes later Sophia came running in.

"Are you okay?" she asked.

"No," I said.

I was standing in front of one of the sinks. I didn't actually throw up, but I didn't feel great.

Then I couldn't help it. Tears started streaming down my face.

"Look," said Sophia. "This isn't that bad. I mean, how many people even know about the site yet? And how many people are like Eric and are going to start clicking through it to find that?"

I thought about that for a second. "Well . . ."

Sophia nodded. "It's fine. You'll talk to your mom after school. She'll fix it."

"Okay," I said, wiping my face. "You're probably right."

I washed my face off with some cold water.

"Fresh as a daisy," I said, and Sophia laughed.

She took out a brush from her bag and fixed my bangs.

"All good," she said.

I gave her a hug and headed to English class.

You know how sometimes you walk into a room and you get this feeling that people are looking at you funny? And usually you figure that you're just being paranoid?

I had that feeling walking into Ms. Parkour's class.

I sat down and noticed that Hannah was looking at me.

What? I mouthed.

She mouthed back, *I get it.*

Get what?

"Okay, class," said Ms. Parkour. "We're going to start off with poetry, then move into a discussion about the writing in your blogs."

For the next twenty minutes we learned about different kinds of poems, which was kind of cool. I had no idea there were so many different kinds, from haiku to a limerick. We had to choose a kind to write.

"Anyone want to venture doing one on the whiteboard?" asked Ms. Parkour.

Eric shot up his hand, and so did Hannah.

"Okay, Eric, batter up," said Ms. Parkour.

"I tried a haiku," he said. "Here goes."

He wrote out his poem on the whiteboard.

Sometimes I feel like
No one ever sees the things
That I think inside.

"Wow," said Ms. Parkour. "That's amazing, Eric!"

I snuck a look at Riley. Our eyebrows shot up.

"So can someone tell me what they think Eric is talking about in this poem?"

"That he sees inside his head!" called out Henry, and everyone laughed.

"Well," said Ms. Parkour, ignoring him. "What is 'seeing inside your head'? Is that your interior thought process?"

"Or your dreams?" asked Hannah.

"Or your dreams," said Ms. Parkour. "Or maybe your inner dialogue? Who has one of those?"

Everyone looked around.

"You all do, right?" asked Ms. Parkour. "That's your inner voice. Like, if you're walking to school and you're thinking, 'Oh, I can't wait to get to English class,' that's your inner voice. So, Eric, can you elaborate on how you're seeing your inner voice?"

"Um," said Eric, suddenly shy.

He squirmed a little in his seat.

"Do you feel like people just assume you're great and things are okay, but maybe you aren't as great as you seem?" asked Hannah.

Eric looked up with a surprised look on his face.

"Yeah," he said. "I mean, that's it exactly."

Hannah nodded. "I feel that way too," she said.

We all turned around and looked at her. Hannah always seemed cheery and really together.

"Okay, Hannah," said Ms. Parkour. "Do you want to tell us what the running theme of your blog is?"

"I guess it's kind of the same as Eric," said Hannah. "I feel like I'm responsible and school is going well and there's nothing really bad to complain about. I have food and a family and friends, but sometimes I just feel kind of . . . ick."

"It's like Kelsey said in her blog," said Eric.

I froze.

"She writes about feeling like a big sigh, and that's just exactly right."

"Kelsey, did you share your blog with Eric?" Ms. Parkour asked, curious.

I was still frozen.

"She shared it with the world," said Eric. "It's online!"

There was some murmuring in the class as Eric directed Ms. Parkour to pull up the blog on the screen.

I still couldn't move.

She glanced back at me, then looked concerned.

"Kelsey, did you post this?"

"No!" I cried, and I couldn't help it, but tears started springing from my eyes. "It was a mistake! It wasn't supposed to be up there!"

Riley jumped up and whispered, "Do you want to go to the restroom?" I looked at her gratefully.

"Ms. Parkour, I think Kelsey needs a little break," said Riley, "so I'm going to walk her down the hall to the restroom."

Ms. Parkour looked worried. "That's a good idea, Riley," she said. "And now, class, let's turn our attention back to what establishes a poem as a haiku."

I could hear her voice trail off as Riley literally marched me out of the room, carrying my bag and hers.

She stopped at the classroom next to ours, and I barely noticed that she was frantically waving to someone inside. Then she steered me into the restroom, where I found myself crying for the second time that day.

"Just let it out," she said.

Two minutes later Molly came slamming in, banging the door against the wall as she opened it.

"What's up?" she said, then stopped suddenly when she saw me crying. "What happened?"

"There's some drama with the donuts," said Riley, and she handed Molly her phone.

"What is this?" asked Molly.

"It's Kelsey's own private blog. She used the template for Kelsey's Kakes, and when that went live, it accidentally also pulled up her blog. People found it. And discussed it in English class."

Molly's eyes bugged out of her head.

"Did the blog talk about me at all?" she asked.

"Molly, for goodness' sake, no," said Riley. "Not really."

"What did it say?" Molly demanded.

"It said I was worried that you'd be mad about the stupid Kelsey's Kakes thing!" I cried, sobbing into my arm.

"Is that all?" asked Molly.

"Molly!" said Riley.

Molly sighed. "Okay, okay, I just wanted to make sure that there wasn't anything about me on there."

Riley gave her a sharp look.

Molly started to read the blog.

"Look," she said, "there's stuff I can see that you don't want anyone to read, but it's not like you talk about anything really personal."

"Those are my thoughts!" I said. "They're private! They weren't meant to be posted online! I never wanted that stupid thing to be named after me! I never wanted the Kelsey's Kakes blog!"

Molly looked at me thoughtfully. "That's actually true," she said. "It wasn't like you had a 'me, me, me' attitude about this. It was kind of pushed on you."

I nodded.

"Okay," said Molly. "Let's put a plan into action here. I'm assuming you can't go back to class in this state."

I looked at her.

"You look like a puffer fish," she said. "No offense." Molly took her phone out of her knapsack.

"What are you doing?" asked Riley.

"Calling for backup," said Molly.

Chapter Fourteen
Out of Business

Molly texted Mom and Dad from the bathroom. She told them what happened.

Mom called her right away, but I wasn't listening. Then Molly announced the plan: I go to the nurse's office and let him know that I had just thrown up.

It was kind of a joke that throwing up was the one thing that got you sent home, no questions asked. I guess they were worried you'd throw up again and they'd have to clean it up.

Molly stood up and said, "Okay, forward march."

Riley and Molly walked me into Mr. Murrow's office, and he took one look at me and said, "Oh, no, something is not right."

"She threw up," said Molly.

"Let's call your parents," said Mr. Murrow.

See? No questions asked.

"Which one is usually able to pick you up during the day?" Mr. Murrow asked.

He then called Mom, who I heard say, "I'm on my way."

"Thanks for your help, Riley and Molly. You should probably head back to class now," said Mr. Murrow.

I saw an odd look cross Molly's face.

"Actually," she said, "I'm not so sure I feel great either. There might be something getting passed around in our family."

I almost giggled, but I was still too upset.

"Okay," said Mr. Murrow. "Let's see what your mom says when she gets here. In the meantime, you two sit on this bench and rest. Riley, let's get you away from your friends in case this is a little contagious. Sometimes stomach bugs are."

"Thanks, Riley," I said. "I'll text you later."

Mr. Murrow gave Riley a pass to return to class. Riley took the pass, nodded, waved, and left the two of us.

The sick bench was where kids sat while they were waiting to be picked up. It was off in a corner of the nurse's office, and there was a little curtain that went around it.

Mr. Murrow closed it and then it was just Molly and me.

"You okay?" asked Molly.

I sniffed. "No," I said, starting to cry again.

"You heard what I told Mom," she said. "I said she should call the website person and take the whole thing down. In a few minutes no one will be able to read anything."

"But they already read it!" I said. "And it was private. That's like the entire class reading your diary!"

"Honestly," said Molly, "a lot of people blog that kind of stuff all the time. They *want* people to read all about what they have to say or think."

"Not me," I said. "If I want to tell you something, I'll say it. I won't post it online. And I definitely don't say things like that to strangers. Why would I want them weighing in?"

"All right, so you won't have a career as a blogger," said Molly.

I blew air out of my mouth hard.

"Why is everyone so focused on what career I'm going to have?"

"They aren't," said Molly.

"But they are!" I said. "Dad is saying I should be a food stylist and Mom is saying I can run Kelsey's Kakes and Nans is saying I'll have a job at the Park. Uncle Mike said I could be a website designer. Now you're adding blogger into the mix."

"Yeah, but people say stuff like that all the time to kids," said Molly. "I'm organized, so a teacher once said I'd be good at designing closets."

"Really?" I said.

"Yeah." Molly shrugged. "I mean, maybe that's a cool job, but . . ."

"Your closet is an absolute mess," I said, shaking my head.

Just then I heard Mom's voice taking to Mr. Murrow, who pulled back the curtain.

"You're both sick?" asked Mom, eyeing Molly.

Molly nodded. "I think I might have the same thing, Mom. I could stay here and see what happens, and try to finish out the day."

"Oh, since you're here and it's already after lunch, maybe you take her home out of an abundance of caution," said Mr. Murrow. "I'll check both of them out for you."

Mom threw a look at Molly and said, "Okay, let's go, girls."

She put her arm around me and we walked out of school. As we headed toward the car, she put her hand on my forehead.

"Mom, she's not really sick," said Molly.

"I know," said Mom. "Reflex. We'll talk about it, but let's get in the car."

As we were pulling out of the parking lot, Dad's car stopped in front of the school, and he flashed his lights.

Mom rolled down the window. "I have both of them," she called.

"Both of them?" Dad asked, and Molly waved from the back seat.

Jenna was in the passenger seat of Dad's car, so I guess we were all headed home early today.

We all went inside and dropped our bags and Dad said, "Okay, family meeting at the kitchen table."

"Can we get a snack before the meeting?" Molly asked.

"I thought you were feeling nauseous," Mom said.

"Yeah, why are you home early, Molly?" Dad asked.

"I'm part of the family, and there's a family

situation going on," said Molly. "Besides, I'm the one who came up with the escape plan for Kelsey. If you come up with the plan, you see it through."

Dad rolled his eyes.

"First things first," said Mom.

She took her laptop out of her work bag and went to the Park site.

"Okay, it's gone," she said. "They took it down."

I peered at the screen. The link to Kelsey's Kakes had been removed.

"How about the link to her blog?" asked Jenna.

"How do you know about that?" I said, exasperated. "Is everyone reading it at the high school too?"

I started to cry.

"I know about it because Dad told me," said Jenna. "Calm down. No one in high school is hanging out on the site for the Park."

I shot her a look.

"Okay, now a snack," said Dad, running his hands through his hair. "Something comforting."

He opened and closed the cabinets.

"Kelsey, is there anything you want?" he asked.

I shook my head.

"I actually might puke," I said.

Ready to Roll!

"Crackers and soup!" said Mom and Dad.

Whenever one of us has an upset stomach, we're served a plate of crackers with some soup.

Mom pulled the box of crackers out of the cabinet, and Dad began defrosting some soup from the freezer. We always have soup in the freezer.

A few minutes later we were all slurping big bowls of chicken soup with crackers on the side. I was actually kind of hungry.

"Now," said Mom. "We have a lot to talk about."

I looked down into my bowl. The steam from the soup felt good hitting my face.

"What happened?" Mom said. "Can you tell me exactly what happened at school?"

"Well," said Molly, "I was in my English class, and I saw Riley jumping up and down in the hallway, and then—"

"Before that," said Mom. "Kelsey, what happened?"

I swallowed hard. "I told Riley and Sophia about the Kelsey's Kakes launch. By lunchtime a lot of kids had already checked it out."

Mom and Dad were watching me closely.

"And by the way, they were all calling me Kelsey Kakes."

I shot an angry glance at Mom, who winced.

"Then we were talking about our blogs in English class. Eric was talking about mine, and Ms. Parkour pulled it up online."

I put my face in my hands and took a deep breath.

"Then everyone in class was reading it. And it was humiliating. Riley got me out of there."

"And Riley motioned to me in the hall," said Molly, "and I met them in the bathroom and came up with the escape plan to get her out of there."

She looked pretty pleased with herself.

"What was this blog?" asked Dad.

"It was an assignment for English class. We were supposed to write a blog about how we were feeling."

"So the blog that posted was about how you were feeling?" asked Dad.

"Yes," I said.

"Kelsey felt like a sigh," said Molly.

"A sigh?" asked Mom. "What does that mean?"

"Like you just don't know what else to do if you're sad or bored or in between, and you just sigh," said Molly. "Right?"

I put my head on the table.

"Why is everyone always talking about me and

not to me?" I wailed. "I am perfectly capable of expressing myself!"

"We know you are," said Mom in her very calm *oh no, we're on the verge of a meltdown and I'm trying to stop it* voice.

I grabbed my napkin and blew my nose.

"She's right," said Jenna. "You kind of rolled over her with the whole Kelsey Kakes plan. She kept saying she didn't want it named after her."

Mom looked surprised. "No," she said. "I had a conversation with Kelsey about it."

"You had a conversation and told her that this was what Grandpa wanted. That's not leaving a whole lot of room for discussion," Jenna said.

"How do you know that's what she said?" I asked, not disputing that was what had happened.

"You can hear everything anyone says in this house," said Jenna.

Her room is right above Mom's office.

"Kelsey, I thought you were okay with this," Mom said.

"I was okay with it but I wasn't thrilled," I said. "I kept saying I didn't like the name. And I'm most upset that it was launched so fast that no one checked the stupid site to see that my other blog was underneath it."

"That was a mistake," said Mom. "And I'm sorry for that. You're right. We should have looked at it thoroughly. The web designer said she's never had that happen before. It was layered on top but hidden pretty well, so she didn't see it."

"It wasn't hidden that well!" I yelped. "Because Eric found it and then everyone else did."

"Can we read the blog?" asked Dad.

"Why not?" I said, throwing up my hands. "Everyone else has."

I reached into my backpack and pulled out my laptop. I opened it, pulled up the original blog, and spun the laptop around.

Mom and Dad huddled together, and I concentrated on my soup.

"You don't want to read it?" Molly asked Jenna.

"I read it in the car on the way home," said Jenna.

I glared.

"What?" she said. "Dad told me about it, so I went on and read it. There really isn't anything overly personal on it, Kels."

"But those are my thoughts, and they were never intended to be shared!" I said. "Only Ms. Parkour was going to read the posts. That's like publishing someone's texts or forwarding an email you meant for one person to a dozen people!"

"All those things happen, unfortunately," said Dad, "so that's a good thing to remember. Whenever you do something electronically, it's difficult to keep it private. That goes for emails, texts, and posts."

"But not documents you save to your own computer!" I yelled.

"Okay, lower your voice, please," said Dad. "And you're absolutely right. But as you can see, sometimes mistakes get made."

"We made a mistake," said Mom. "And you got hurt. And I can't even tell you how terrible I feel about that, Kelsey. It was a mistake, sure, and nobody meant to do this to you regarding your blog, but obviously we all rolled way too fast on this whole project, and you were the one who paid the price."

Her phone buzzed.

"It's still work hours, so let me just check that," she said.

She read the text and made a face.

"What should we do next to make you feel better, Kelsey?" she asked.

"It's all erased, right? There's no way for anyone to see it anymore or get to it?"

Mom nodded. "The web designer checked, I checked, and Uncle Mike and Uncle Charlie checked on their phones, their computers, and their tablets, just to make sure."

"Oh, great," I said. "So the whole family read the blog?"

"Nans did," said Mom. "She actually thinks you're quite expressive. She said maybe you'll be a writer or a poet."

I slammed my fist down on the table.

"I do not want to be a poet!" I said. "And I'm so very sick of people suggesting what I might be when I have to work as an adult!"

Mom looked at Dad.

"I suggested a food stylist career the other day," said Dad.

"And we thought maybe you'd want to work at Kelsey's Kakes," said Mom.

"And Nans thought I should work at the Park!" I yelled. "I already work at the Park! I'm twelve! Only twelve! Sometimes I feel blah. I don't like rain! But I will figure it out! I don't know that I positively want to stay here forever. I don't know for certain that field hockey is the only sport for me like soccer is for Molly. I'm figuring it out! Let me figure it out!"

It takes a lot to get complete silence in my family, but that speech managed to do it.

"She has a point," said Molly, finally.

Mom looked like she was about to cry. Dad looked like he didn't know what to say.

Mom's phone kept buzzing.

"Is there some emergency?" Dad asked.

"No," said Mom grimly. "Those are orders coming in for Kelsey's Kakes. We have over a dozen orders so far."

I pushed my chair away from the table.

"Tell them you can't do it," I said. "Because Kelsey's Kakes is out of business."

Chapter Fifteen
Seven Cousins Cakes

I flopped onto my bed. I realized that I had left my laptop downstairs, along with my phone, so I couldn't even email or text any of my friends.

I took out a piece of paper. Maybe this was the best way to do a blog after all. This way nobody could post it online. I grabbed a pen and started to write.

Maybe it's worse to feel raging angry than just blah. When you feel blah, you aren't feeling too much in either direction. You aren't too angry, you aren't too sad, you aren't too frustrated. Being in the middle might not be terrible.

I thought about that for a minute.

As I was twirling the pen around, Molly poked her head in.

"You know," she said, "I was never angry at you."

"Okay," I said.

"I wasn't," said Molly. "I was angry at Mom because I thought it wasn't fair, but it wasn't your fault. And you're my sister. It was a great idea, and I'd always support new things you did. Or old things you do. I'd just support you."

"Okay," I said. "Thanks. And thanks for getting me out of there today."

"Vomit," said Molly, shrugging. "Vomit scares them every time."

I realized that since we came home early, I still had hours to go until dinner, so I cleaned out one of my drawers, I painted nail polish on my toes, and then I doodled all over my sketch pad.

I was wondering what Mom and Dad's plan was. Were they both going to come up here or were they going to wait until we all sat down to dinner? I knew this obviously wasn't over.

After I doodled for a while, I sketched out a few things. I stood back and looked at one design. I liked it. A lot.

Then Mom called us for dinner, and as usual, it meant I had to drop everything and get down to the kitchen.

Dinner was weird. It was weird because it was normal.

Mom and Dad asked Molly and Jenna about their days at school. I noticed they didn't do "best and worst" part of the day, but I guess that would have just been asking to rehash my misery.

After dinner we had bowls of ice cream. I wondered if Mom and Dad were just waiting me out on this.

Jenna asked to be excused to go finish her homework, and then Molly did too. I looked up.

"Can I be excused too?" I asked.

"We'd like to talk to you first," said Dad.

And there it was.

"Good luck!" Molly called, as she scooted upstairs.

"I'm not sure why she's wishing you good luck," said Dad. "You aren't in trouble."

"In fact, we'd like to apologize to you," said Mom. "I clearly didn't listen to you about the donut cakes. Or I didn't listen hard enough, and for that I apologize. And I apologize for the mistake we made in publishing your blog. That must have felt awful. I would never do anything to intentionally hurt one of my daughters and yet, I did."

"And," said Dad, "we want to apologize for making you feel like we felt you couldn't figure out a path for yourself. Of course you can. You are smart and capable and have many different talents. And if you don't know for a while what you want to become, that's fine. Some adults still don't know. Or some think they do and change their mind later on."

"Okay," I said. "So what about Kelsey's Kakes?"

"I'm going to talk to Uncle Mike and Grandpa about it tomorrow," said Mom. "I think we should put this whole plan on hold. And we will never repost that blog. Either blog."

I thought about that. "There were some ideas on that Kelsey's Kakes blog that were kind of good."

"They were great," Mom agreed. "But we can move on."

"Wait here," I said. "I want to show you something."

I ran up to my room and grabbed my sketch pad.

"This," I said, spreading out a page on the table, "seems cool to me."

I had drawn a new logo with the words *Seven Cousins Cakes* in different lettering from the original Kelsey's Kakes blog on top of a donut cake.

"Seven Cousins Cakes?" asked Mom.

"There are seven of us," I said. "Me, Molly, Jenna, Lindsay and Sky, and Rich and Lily."

"Yes," said Mom. "But I'm not following you. What is this?"

"The new logo," I said. "Let's call it Seven Cousins Cakes. That way it's named after all of us. And that way," I added, "it's totally up for grabs as to who runs it later."

Mom smiled.

"What do you think, Chris?" she asked Dad, who was wiping a tear away with his napkin.

"Oh, I think it's just perfect," he said. "All the cousins . . ."

"Dad, you are such a mush," I said, laughing.

"So you're okay with us going ahead?" asked Mom.

"I think so," I said, "as long as it's not really about me. I'd like to see this work. And you said you had orders, right?"

Mom nodded. "They're pouring in. A lot of fairy cake orders!"

I smiled. "Olivia had a great idea for a butterfly cake," I said.

"Ooh," said Mom. "I love that."

"So," I said, "if we call this Seven Cousins Cakes and take my name and my picture off everything, I can still help out with the blog if you'd like. We'll just make sure to put it in a brand-new template to avoid any potential issues with copying."

"I promise we'll triple-check it," Mom said. "And for what it's worth, I think Grandpa will love the new name."

"I think it's a great name!" called Jenna.

"Jenna, are you in your room?" Dad called back.

"Yep!" she yelled. "I told you I could hear everything in this house!"

Chapter Sixteen
Family Toast

I had to go to school the next day, but at least it wasn't raining and it wasn't freezing cold.

Riley and Sophia knew how nervous I was, so they were waiting for me outside of school, which made me feel so much better.

Molly walked up to the door with me, then bowed in front of them, made a big sweep of her arm, and said, "And here's the handoff. Riley and Sophia, I hand you the very fragile Kelsey. Please make sure Eric stays away from her today."

We all cracked up, but the plan worked.

Or maybe Riley and Sophia had already told everyone to back off, because no one mentioned the blog at all.

In English class I got lucky, since Ms. Parkour was out, and there was a substitute who just had us do some extra reading.

"It's Friday," Riley whispered to me, leaning across the aisle. "Everyone forgets everything over the weekend. You'll be golden by Monday."

I was actually a little excited to go to Donut Dreams after school. I bounded into the Park, heading straight for the kitchen so I could put on my apron and get to work.

I noticed that the kitchen seemed busier than usual until I realized that all the cousins were working one shift, which was weird.

Uncle Charlie, Uncle Mike, and Mom worked at the Park every day with Grandpa and Nans, but the cousins usually had different shifts, and it was actually pretty rare that we were all there together.

I noticed even Skylar, who usually only visited for a few minutes while he was waiting for Uncle Mike to take him somewhere, was sitting at a counter, coloring, with a plate of grilled cheese in front of him.

"Hi, Sky," I said.

"Hi, Cousin Kelsey," he said.

Sky thought it was funny to call me Cousin Kelsey. I guess it was a thing that ran in the family that they liked to use my name in funny ways.

At least he didn't call me Kelsey Kakes.

Before the dinner shift there was sometimes a staff meeting in the kitchen, where they'd go over the specials for the night or give the staff a heads-up about big parties coming in.

Grandpa hit a knife on the side of a glass as a sort of bell for them, and he was doing it now, which was weird because it was still early to think about dinner, unless you were Mrs. Shah, who came in every day at four o'clock for dinner.

"I need the following staff, please," said Grandpa. "Rich, Lily, Jenna, Molly, Kelsey, Lindsay, and Skylar."

"Hey, I don't work here yet!" said Sky.

"You will when you're old enough," said Grandpa.

We huddled around Grandpa, Nans, Mom, Uncle Mike, and Uncle Charlie.

"This is like Thanksgiving," said Sky. "We're all here!"

"Yes," said Grandpa. "And there's nothing I like more than having my family around. So without much fuss and fanfare, I wanted to announce the official opening this weekend of our new business."

He nodded to Mom and Uncle Mike.

Mom held what looked like a big roll of paper. Uncle Mike unrolled it, and it was a huge sign that said SEVEN COUSINS CAKES with the logo I'd drawn, and it had a picture of one of the donut cakes on it.

"Our new venture is named after my seven most favorite, most loved people in the world," said Grandpa. "All my grandchildren."

"Hey, Dad!" said Uncle Charlie. "You also have three kids."

Grandpa waved his hand. "This new business is for a new generation at the Park. This is a family business, run by family, for families. And if anyone in our family would like to join us, they're always welcome."

He glanced at me and smiled.

"And if they only want to come back for donuts, that's okay too," he said.

We all laughed.

"So as a toast to this new venture with our family, let's toast the best way possible."

He turned and gestured to Nans, who rolled in a little table with a tablecloth on it.

On top of the table was a huge donut cake, with little 7's all over it made out of icing. At the bottom of the cake there were outlines of seven kids in different colors of frosting. It almost looked like a set of cutout paper dolls, all holding hands.

"This is a sweet toast," said Grandpa. "Everyone has a glass of lemonade. Please raise them."

We all raised our glasses.

Grandpa continued, "To my very lucky seven grandchildren who will share the sweetest namesake I can think of . . . a business consisting of cakes that are built to make everyone happy."

"Hear, hear!" said Uncle Mike.

Then Grandpa looked around and said, "Now when did I ever have to ask any of my grandchildren if they wanted a donut?"

Then he stepped back, and we all lunged for one. Skylar grabbed two, one with each hand.

Mom put her arm around me. "How do you feel?" she asked.

"Pretty good," I said. "I'm actually feeling creative. I'm thinking of stacking a few hamburgers and seeing where that might go."

Mom laughed.

"You never know," she said. "Grandpa loves new ideas."

"Especially when they come from one of his favorite seven grandchildren," I said, with a smile.

I took a bite. My family was right about one thing: a donut always makes you feel better at the end of the day.

Still Hungry?
Here's a taste of the seventh book in the

series, **Donut Goals!**

Chapter One
Running Is the Best Thing

Riiiiing!!!

I jumped out of my seat and grabbed my backpack, which was hanging from my chair. School was finally out!

Hoisting my backpack across my shoulders, I ran out the door and hurried to my locker. Even though I like my classes and can sit still and pay attention during them, my legs are always itching to leave by the end of the day.

I know that I left recess behind in elementary school, but there's part of me that really wishes that I could have brought it with me into middle school.

I love the idea of being able to go out into the sunshine after a few hours of classes and stretch and run. I would ignore the tetherballs and basketball hoops and make a beeline for the group of kids playing tag.

In the short time we had outside, I'd run and duck and swerve, sometimes getting close to the tagger, then spinning around and flying toward the "safe" wall of the school building.

I loved the feeling of excitement of outrunning somebody, or dodging their outstretched hand as I bolted across the playground.

I've got gym class scheduled, but it's only once a week and it never feels like enough exercise.

I am lucky, though—there is one sport that I've been playing for six years that helps me feel happy in my body. Mom and Dad signed me up for soccer when I was in kindergarten, and I've been playing ever since.

I love the way it feels when I'm totally concentrated on the ball, dribbling and passing and moving it forward to the opposing team's goal. Even though my body is working hard, it's a special moment when my head gets really quiet as it focuses on the next play.

Run, dribble, pass, repeat, score!

I had soccer practice the next day, but today I was walking home with my sister Kelsey. I found her by the front of the school, and together we started on our way.

Kelsey and I are really close in age, but we don't share a lot of things in common.

For one thing, Mom and Dad are Kelsey's birth mother and father, while I was adopted by them from South Korea when I was just a baby.

Kelsey looks like a combination of my parents, with her light brown hair and green eyes, while I've got straight black hair and dark brown eyes.

My sister is super disorganized, while I like to keep track of all my things. (Don't look in my closet, though—it is the one part of my life that I allow to go a little haywire.)

Kelsey also isn't always on time, while I hate it when I'm even a minute late for things.

But despite our differences, I love having Kelsey as a sister. And I feel protective of her too.

When her personal blog accidentally got posted to the web, even though there wasn't anything really sensitive that she shared, I made a plan to get her out of school that day and home with Mom and Dad so she didn't have to be around the kids who had just read her innermost thoughts.

I think that helping her drew the two of us closer together.

"Want to go for a run when we get home?" I asked Kelsey as we walked along. "It's the perfect weather for it."

I held my finger in the air as if I was testing it. The air was sharp and crisp, cool, but not the kind of cool that makes you want to stay inside.

Kelsey shook her head. "Nah. I'm reading a really good book, and I'm almost done with it. I want to see what happens in the end."

She shrugged her shoulders, adjusting her backpack.

"Plus, I feel like I haven't been paying enough attention to Rusty lately. I kind of feel like snuggle time is on the horizon."

I nodded.

Rusty is the dog we'd adopted. One of our

neighbors, Mrs. Rose, helps out at a local rescue shelter, fostering dogs until they're adopted so they don't have to be kept in the shelter's kennels all the time.

One day Mrs. Rose was walking by my soccer practice with a couple of dogs that she was fostering, and that's when I saw Rusty. He was really shy, and I was immediately drawn to how he seemed to be so scared of the world but became happy and playful when showered with attention.

Mrs. Rose had named him Rusty for his reddish-brown fur, and she told me that a hiker had found him abandoned in the woods, hiding under some rocks.

It took some convincing, but eventually Mom and Dad decided that having a dog in the house would be a great addition to the family, and we adopted Rusty.

I quickly found out that adopting a cute dog is a lot more work than actually taking care of one— Rusty needs to be walked twice a day, and picking up his poop is never fun.

But whenever he hops up onto my bed and curls up into a bagel to take a nap, I have to grin at how much I love him. And even though I'm cleaning up after him constantly, I wouldn't trade him for anything.

Rusty is the family dog, though, and if Kelsey wanted to spend some time with him, that was awesome.

"All right," I told Kelsey. "Maybe Jenna will want to go for a run with me."

Jenna is my older sister. She mostly keeps to her own group of friends, but every once in a while she'll hang out with Kelsey and me.

When we got home, Rusty was waiting for us at the door. After wrapping him in a giant hug and rubbing his furry head while he wagged his tail happily, I took off my school shoes and padded in socks to the kitchen, where Dad was waiting for us with after-school snacks.

"I present to you ... apple nachos!" he said proudly, displaying a plate covered in thinly cut apples slices arranged carefully in a spiral. He had drizzled peanut butter, honey, and granola over them.

"Cool!" I washed my hands with soap and water, then picked up a slice and gobbled it up.

"This is great, Dad!" I mumbled as I picked up three more slices and fit them all in my mouth.

"Agreed," Kelsey said, her mouth equally full.

"Did you get this recipe from Grandpa and Nans?" I asked, licking peanut butter off my finger.

My grandparents are both really talented cooks and have owned a restaurant called the Park View Table in our little town of Bellgrove since basically forever.

It's a family operation, with pretty much all my relatives helping out in one way or another—including Kelsey, Jenna, and me.

I've got three cousins who also work there, and together we make sure that the floors are swept, the tables are bused, the orders are right, and that things run as smoothly as possible.

My grandmother's specialty is donuts, and years ago she created a counter inside the restaurant called Donut Dreams that my uncle Mike runs now.

Nans has always had a way of making something ordinary extraordinary—like taking a chocolate donut and making it extra chocolatey by adding a chocolate glaze and chocolate cream inside.

Anyway, I figured that if my dad was sprucing up our snacks, he must have gotten it from a secret family recipe.

"Nope," Dad said, surprising me. "I got it off the old Internet."

"Well, these apple nachos are still delicious, even if it wasn't something that was handed down over generations. Thanks, Dad!" I said.

I downed the rest of my snack and went to my room to change. On my way, I stopped by the living room, where I found Jenna in front of the TV, watching a movie and eating popcorn.

"Hey, Jenna. Want to go on a run with me?" I asked hopefully.

"Nope." Jenna's eyes were glued to the screen, where a pretty exciting car chase was happening. "I would never keep up."

I laughed. "Of course you would. You're, like, at least three inches taller than I am."

"Doesn't matter," said Kelsey, coming into the room with Rusty at her heels. "You're way too fast for the both of us, Molly."

"Yeah, plus running is no fun at all," Jenna said. "It's just flopping one foot in front of the other over and over again. It's monotonous and boring."

I winced.

I've heard this argument before. I can't say that

running is the most glamorous of things to be doing on a Monday afternoon.

"I know it can look boring," I told my sisters. "But it's really important for me to stay in shape for soccer, and running is the best thing I can do to make sure that I'm competitive on the field."

Jenna shot me a look that definitely had a big-sister-does-not-want-to-be-bothered air to it.

"Molly, I really appreciate that you love soccer. I really do. But I'm not going on a run, and right now I want to watch my movie."

"All right," I sighed, and headed upstairs with Kelsey.

"Hey, Molly," Kelsey said as she paused in front of her bedroom door. "You know, I really admire how dedicated you are to soccer."

I had been feeling pretty glum at Jenna being annoyed at me, but Kelsey's words cheered me up.

"You do?"

"Yeah." Kelsey grinned. "You've got a lot of perseverance. And even though I am also not ever going to go running with you, it's really awesome that you're doing something that you love."

"Thanks, Kelsey." I impulsively gave her a hug.

"Soccer does mean a lot to me. One day I'm hoping that it'll get me a sports scholarship into college. Stanford or University of North Carolina would be great, but I would settle for UCLA if I had to."

"Well, while you figure out your life plans five years from now, I'm going to go read my book."

Kelsey hugged me back, then went into her room, while I went into mine.

I changed into my running shorts—pale pink with black stripes—and a dark green sleeveless shirt. Even though it was fall, I loved the feeling of the wind on my shoulders when I was outside and pumping my legs as hard as I could.

I used a scrunchie to tie my hair back into a long ponytail, then went downstairs to grab a big glass of water.

After gulping it down, I yelled out to my dad, who was in the living room with Jenna. "I'm going for a run!"

"Have fun, sweetie," he called back.

I went to the front door and pulled my running sneakers from the shoe cubby. I sat down and laced up them up.

I loved this part right before I headed out the door.

I liked to get the tension of the laces just right against my feet, tight but not too tight, until each sneaker felt like it was an extension of my own foot.

I stood up, checked the time, then headed out.

On the front steps I breathed in the cool air while I did a couple of stretches. Then I took off at an easy jog. After a couple of minutes, I gradually increased my pace, feeling my heart rate ramp up.

By the time I reached the track, I could feel my heart pounding. There was sweat rolling down the sides of my temples, and despite the chill air, I was warm.

My foot hit the rubber of the track, and like a switch that had suddenly been flipped on, I burst into my highest gear. I glided across the ground, feeling only my body and my heart and my determination as I pushed myself to the limit.

What I love about running is that there comes a moment, after all the groans and protests that your muscles make, when everything seems to melt away. Your mind quiets, and while you're still working like crazy to run, it all feels effortless and beautiful.

I finished my run and checked my time on my watch.

I'd run an eight-minute mile!

It was one of the best times I had ever gotten. I felt excited and happy and strong.

In a lot of ways, running for me was a means to an end. It steadied me, and I liked how it was part of my daily life. But I mostly ran because it helped me with my stamina while playing soccer, which was absolutely the most important thing in my life besides family.

And I was going to need a lot of stamina soon. My soccer team was having a really big match in two weeks, and I had to be in tip-top shape if I wanted our team to have a chance at winning!

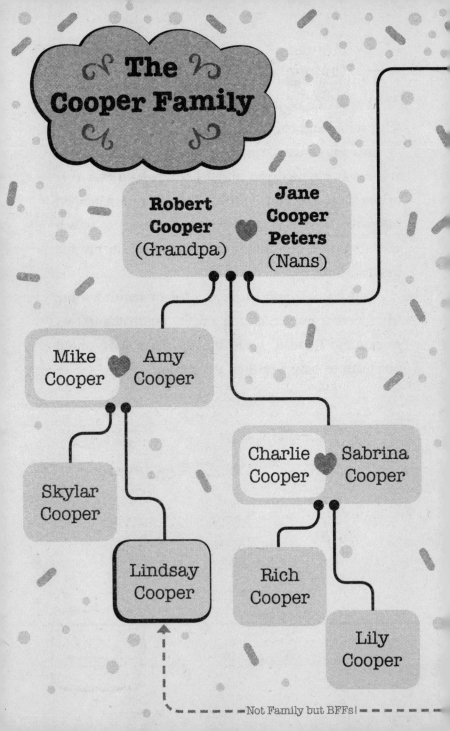

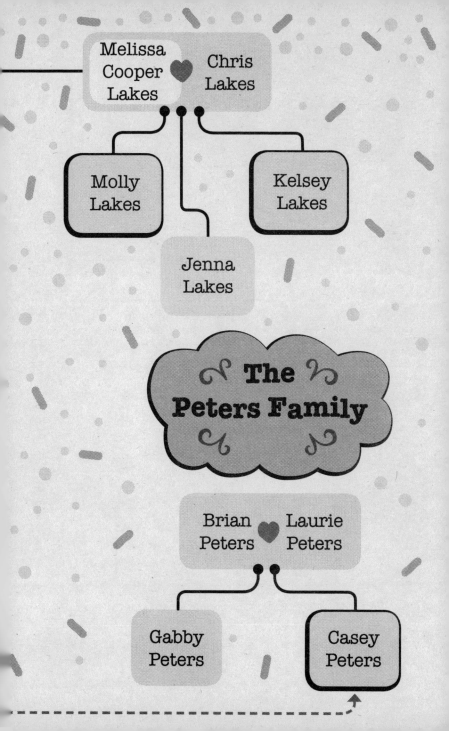

Melissa Cooper Lakes ♥ Chris Lakes

Molly Lakes

Kelsey Lakes

Jenna Lakes

The Peters Family

Brian Peters ♥ Laurie Peters

Gabby Peters

Casey Peters